DESTINED HEARTS

Three Hearts 3

Tonya Ramagos

MENAGE AMOUR

Siren Publishing, Inc.
www.SirenPublishing.com

A SIREN PUBLISHING BOOK
IMPRINT: Ménage Amour

DESTINED HEARTS
Copyright © 2009 by Tonya Ramagos

ISBN-10: 1-60601-437-4
ISBN-13: 978-1-60601-437-0

First Printing: June 2009

Cover design by Jinger Heaston
All cover art and logo copyright © 2009 by Siren Publishing, Inc.

Printed in the U.S.A.

PUBLISHER
Siren Publishing, Inc.
www.SirenPublishing.com

DEDICATION

To my readers. May you find all you desire in your destined heart.

DESTINED HEARTS

Three Hearts 3

TONYA RAMAGOS
Copyright © 2009

Chapter One

Calliope felt the warmth radiate from his body pressed to hers and sighed as the pleasure moved through her, as the thrill sizzled in her veins. He gazed down at her through eyes darker than the deepest depths of the universe, the expression on his flawlessly handsome face one of utter love and complete devotion. Her heart flipped excitedly in her chest, her stomach alive with dozens of tiny butterflies, and her core afire with sexual delight as his lips closed over hers in a kiss so light, so lovely it stole her breath.

"The people are arriving early tonight and a slew of them, too. Look at all of them!"

Calliope blinked, the image of the dark, striking stranger vanishing as she caught sight of her sister in the mirror. Karan stood at the window, her back to the bedchamber. There was tension in her strong shoulders, Calliope noted even as she envied the play of muscles left exposed by the strapless siren red dress. It was a dress one would never see in the lands of the Gods. But, then again, her sister was of a different land now, a different time. It was the power she possessed that gave her the ability to travel between those worlds.

"The third daughter of their goddess queen shall find the man of her heart's desire on this night. It is a moment not to be missed."

Aithne's words spoken with as much trepidation as excitement drew Calliope's attention to her oldest sister. A woman definitely fit for the land of the Gods, she perched on the edge of the bed, one hand absently caressing her slightly rounded belly covered by a dress of soft green that oddly accented rather than clashed with her tumble of fiery red hair.

"It is a moment for them to gawk, to pry, to gossip." Karan sneered as she turned from the window, her long dark hair swinging like a curtain over one shoulder. She pitched her voice to that of a stage whisper and cupped a hand around her mouth as if speaking secretively to another. "I wonder who it shall be. Look at the way he looks at her. Oh, do you not think he would be the perfect match for her?" She rolled her eyes and tipped her head back at the window. "They are probably whispering about it already, speculating."

"Karan, it is the way of our land, our people." Aithne gave a long winded sigh. "You know this. We have been through this twice already."

"That does not make it anymore…"

Calliope tuned out, focusing on her own reflection in the mirror as her sisters bickered quietly. She was considered by all in their lands to be the most beautiful of the three demigoddess daughters born to the Goddess Queen Ina and King Andrew. With hair that shimmered like sunlight, eyes the delicate blue of cornflowers, and skin as soft and flawless as whipped cream, she often saw herself as too delicate, too dainty, too shy. How she longed for Aithne's contrasting beauty and sense of adventure; or Karan's unconventional, almost boyish muscular physic and unyielding bravery.

Instead, she had been given the beauty of a rose, the stability of its stem in a winter chill, and the heart of a timid but ever hopeful romantic. Karan would say hopeless romantic, Calliope mused and disagreed. She was very hopeful and immensely excited to find her love. Aithne had been right. This night was a moment. This night she would finally, at long last, find the man of her heart's desire, her destined mate to whom she would join forever.

"Tell me again how it feels." She turned from the mirror to face her sisters, her quietly spoken request putting an instant end to their squabbling. "Describe to me again what I shall feel inside when first my eyes meet with his. You know. Both of you have felt it." And both were now joined with the men of their destinies. Jealousy curled in her belly like a poisonous snake. It was all she wanted her whole life, all she ever dreamed, and all she lived for. To find her true love, join with him, and live with him forever.

Her handsome stranger with the fathomless black eyes tore to the forefront of her mind as he so often had for as long as she could remember. It seemed he had always been there, drifting in her thoughts, her dreams, waiting for her to find him. Well, it was generally her dark-eyed love, though sometimes those eyes turned a brilliant sparkling green. But always he came as strong, mystifying, and arousing. As a young girl, she fantasized he would sweep her off her feet, carry her to a marvelous castle on a mountain top where they would forever live in happiness and the blinding light of love. As a woman, well, her fantasies had not changed much but for the intimacy, the longing only maturity could bring.

"It is a feeling in your belly as mother described to me the night of my joining celebration." Aithne's green and gold flecked eyes turned dreamy as she remembered. "It is a quake, a tremble that possesses the heart and the mind. A quiver down to your toes of a power the likes of which you have never before felt nor will ever feel in the presence of any other. It hurts and excites, terrifies and pleases. Mother was right. It is all of that and more. So much more."

"Was that the way of it for you, too?" Calliope turned her attention to Karan. Of the three of them, her middle sister had been the one determined to never mate. She fought, denied, and refused until nearly the bitter end even after she met her destined heart. When Karan answered, it surprised her.

"It was and so much more. What Aithne fails to mention is the rush of heat to your breasts, the throb between your legs." Karan began to laugh as Calliope felt her eyes grow wide.

She had felt those things, knew of the desires of the body, the pleasures of the flesh but... "Is it not lust you speak of?"

"Of course it is lust," Karan said. "You should find the man of your heart as easy to lust after as to love, do you not think? You cannot tell me that sappy fantasy you have had all your life never made it to the bedchamber." She waggled her eyebrows and grinned suggestively.

"No, I cannot." Calliope felt her cheeks heat. Because she tired of the way her sisters so often thought of her as the innocent, good girl, she shot them a wicked smile. "My fantasies always make it to the bedchamber after extended stops in the hallway, the great room, the grand dining room, the staircase, the—"

"Okay, okay." Karan threw back her head and hooted with laughter.

"To use Karan's favorite otherworldly expression, you go girl." Aithne joined in the laughter, shaking her head.

"Do not go through with it tonight." Karan's sudden, so serious tone had the sound of laughter in the chamber dying a quick death.

Stunned, Calliope stared at her sister. "You wish me to miss my own joining celebration?"

"I want you to be safe." Karan rushed to her, knelt on her knees in front of her, and took her hands. "I am scared for you, Calliope."

Karan's voice wobbled ever so slightly, but it was the words she spoke that had Calliope's eyes brimming with tears. Her heart raced from a bone deep terror. Karan was the strong one of the three, the brave one. She was not supposed to be scared of anything! Though Calliope knew Karan had been. When the bad guys took her in the alternate world, Karan had surely been frightened then. And had she not been petrified to join with her true mate, to place her heart in the hands of a man?

"You would have me cancel the celebration on this night?" Calliope's gaze flicked to Aithne and she saw the echoing sentiment in her eldest sister's expression. "Even if I wished to do so, such a thing cannot be done."

"It can." The quiet words drew Calliope's attention to the doorway of the bedchamber. Her mother, the Goddess Queen Ina, stood with her hands clasped tightly together, her face a carving of worry and fear. "I can send our people home; order the celebration not to be held. All you must do is say the word and I shall do as you wish."

"You would not do it for Karan." And Karan had wanted nothing more than to flee her celebration a mere phase of the moon's time ago. "You said it was her duty, her place as your daughter. You said the celebration is custom in our land, has been for more millennia than any of us have lived. All who are heir to the goddess throne have such an event when they come of age and you would not cancel it no matter how much we fear the outcome."

"Your memory, my youngest beauty, is as always impeccable." Ina sighed as she stepped closer. The skirt of her royal gown made a soft swishing sound around her slim ankles as she walked.

She might call Calliope her beauty, but even her youngest daughter's loveliness paled in comparison to the queen. Hair of a glimmering gold with eyes that were an undetermined shade somewhere between green, blue and gray, shapely lips and even shapelier curves, the queen exuded power, delicacy, and femininity from every pore.

"I did say all of that and likely more." Ina stopped behind Calliope. The hands she rested on Calliope's shoulders were stiff, cold, and just a bit shaky. She met Calliope's gaze in the mirror. "It is different for you. Perhaps I should have been willing to change my stand for your sisters. Perhaps not. As it turned out, in the end all was for the best. I wish I could believe it would be so for you as well."

"But you cannot. You are more afraid for me than you were for them." The chilly fingers of that fear danced along her spine. The eyes that met hers in the mirror, her mother's eyes, swirled with emotions she never thought to see on the queen's face.

"It is the spell cast upon you that is the most horrid," Aithne reminded. "You are fated to be engulfed by a world of darkness, to reside in terror and face a monster that will bring a death of no end."

Calliope was not the only one with an impeccable memory. Aithne spoke the words of the spell word for soul chilling word. A curse put upon the three of them at birth by their grandmother and, at that time, reigning goddess queen, Daria. A spell that fated each of them to face matters of the heart that inevitably led to their deaths. Except, Aithne and Karan met their hearts, fought against their parts of the spell and triumphed, gaining not only the hearts of their destined mates, but powers neither had possessed before. Aithne now held the power to heal; Karan had the power to travel through a door between worlds long ago sealed for all eternity.

"You faced the demons of your spells and you came through them unharmed. You think me too fragile, too slight."

"Calliope, we do not think—"

"You do, Aithne. And you are likely right in part. I do not hold your sense of adventure, your enthusiasm of the quest. I am not brave and rebellious as you are, Karan. What I am is a woman who wishes for love, a family, a home. I wish to fulfill my duty as the demigoddess daughter of a love goddess."

"The threats we faced were not nearly as huge." Karan shook her head and squeezed Calliope's hands. "Aithne and I came against death, yes, but monsters, darkness, terror…those horrors were not part of our spell."

"Perhaps they are not words of literal sense, but metaphorical as yours turned out to be. It has all come down to matters of the heart so far, choices that have proven the curse can be broken. Aithne desired two men and, in the end, had to choose between them, to recognize which held her true heart to break her spell and heal herself of the poison within her. Your heart was divided, between the man you were fated to love and your own stubborn desire not to love anyone. Then you were torn between his world and ours. Only when you finally gave into your heart, gave into *him*, found yourself willing to give up your world for him, did you break your spell and gain the power to travel between his world and ours."

"But what if the words are literal this time?" Karan asked, her lavender eyes imploring. "What if it is different for you?"

"You fear the terror, the darkness." She met each of her sister's gazes in turn, and then settled on her mother's in the mirror. "As do I. But do you not see that love, true love, shines through any dark? It is what I have wanted my whole life. This night is what I have waited for." Determination, defiance, and a boldness she never before felt surged through her veins. She squared her shoulders, lifted her chin, and met her own gaze in the mirror. "I will have my celebration, I will meet my true heart, and I will face whatever I must to break the spell once and for all."

"You are wrong, little sister." A single tear slid down Karan's cheek. "You are the brave one."

* * * *

"We should not be here." Reinn scowled as men and women, Fae and faerie, sprites and nymphs passed. Most moved by without notice. Some shot him sidelong glances. Did they know who he was? *What* he was?

"I have to be here." Bronwen kept with his steady pace toward the palace of the goddess queen. His muscular legs clad in black leather carried him in long, even strides. His booted feet crunched on the pebbled walk with each step. His broad shoulder encased in a crisp white shirt with white lace lapels brushed a passerby, but his attention was oblivious to the visible chill the woman experienced at the light contact, to the look of abject fear that leapt into her eyes.

"And what do you intend to do? Will you waltz into that palace, take the hand of the queen's daughter and tango your way back out?" Reinn's sarcasm was not lost on Bronwen. When the other man turned, his lips tilting in an amused grin, Reinn felt his loins tense, his blood pumping hot and excitedly in his veins. He loved that look on Bronwen's face, so mischievous, so wicked, and so sexy.

"It is a thought." Bronwen finally slowed and moved to one side of the gathering crowd making their way through the double doors of the goddess queen's palace.

"A damned stupid one," Reinn muttered. "She will not want you." *But I do.*

Bronwen fisted Reinn's shirt in his hand, lifted his feet inches off the ground, and slammed him against the stone wall of the palace so fast Reinn didn't see it coming. Reinn's breath left him on a whoosh of painful surprise as the blow reverberated through his body. Bronwen possessed strength to rival any man, any beast and Reinn figured he felt only a fraction of that force now.

"She will want me." Bronwen spit the words in Reinn's face. "She has no choice but to want me. It is her way, her tradition, her duty. She is the daughter of a love goddess, a Queen, and I am her destined heart. It is no simpler than that."

Reinn closed his eyes and slowly nodded. The agony in Bronwen's gaze tore at his heart even as the anger in Bronwen's voice tightened his balls, hardened his cock. He wanted to comfort, to sooth, to ease the anguish in Bronwen's mesmerizing eyes, but how did he do so for a man who loved another? They had been together for decades, both living a life of predatory darkness and solitude. And in all those decades, Reinn knew Bronwen's heart belonged not to him. Some believed a creature of the Underworld possessed no heart. Some were wrong.

"I am thinking only of you," Reinn said when Bronwen's grip on his shirt slowly loosened, when he felt his feet ease back to solid ground. "I don't wish to see you hurt, my friend. What you are after tonight is only madness."

"I am doing what I have to do." Bronwen stepped back, but the fury, the torment remained in his pitch black eyes. "You know. You have always known."

Reinn nodded. "As you have always known you cannot go through with this. You cannot have her."

* * * *

She did not feel so brave. Tension jittered in Calliope's stomach making her grateful she had not taken the time to eat since breakfast. Her hand on her father's arm tightened and she fought to keep her breaths even, steady. Hyperventilating until she became lightheaded and toppled head over heels down the stone staircase would do her no good.

"Is it excitement or nerves?" Her father leaned in and brushed a kiss to her cheek with lips that smiled in amusement.

"Does nothing get by you?" Calliope looked up at her father, into his all-knowing eyes the color of smoky rain clouds. *So handsome.* She always thought so. His hair was a deep tree bark brown that fell in a satiny curtain around a face lightly creased with lines around the eyes and lips. Character lines as she often thought of them.

Andrew shook his head. "Not when it concerns one of my daughters."

Calliope gave a shaky laugh. "I am not certain. Both, I suppose."

"You have waited for this night your whole life." Understanding sparked with obvious memories like lightning bolts in his eyes. "I believe you were born searching for your mate."

"As do I. Do you worry too, father?" She knew he did. She had only to see his expression, to feel the worry radiating from his body.

"Of course I worry. It is my job as your father, as the king to worry."

"I wish you would not." She wanted to hug him, to hold him close. More, she longed to curl in his lap like she did as a young girl. Yet, even then she dreamed of her mate, of this night, of the customary celebration. He was right. She had been born searching for her true heart.

"Your mother said you refused to cancel the celebration. She would do it for you without regard to opinions or laws."

"She should not." Calliope lowered her voice, careful to be sure only her father heard her. She need not turn to know her mother stood a discrete distance behind her, Karan and Aithne at her side. "As queen she should have more care for those opinions and laws."

"Ah, but it is her disregard for such laws, as well as my own, that led us here."

Calliope shook her head. "Canceling tonight's gala would not be right. It would not be fair. It would not be destiny."

"It would certainly disappoint all of them." His gaze flicked to the crowd of people gathered around the bottom of the grand staircase, the scattering of others throughout the grand ballroom.

Calliope stared into faces, studied features, and felt her heart thump then sigh each time her gaze locked with a handsome male in the crowd. In nights passed, she had envisioned this moment, pictured herself dashing down the stone stairs and launching herself into the arms of her destined mate. Too easy, too instant, she told herself when she felt none of the bone deep quiver she longed for with each transfixed gaze.

"Then they shall not be disappointed." She looked back at her father and smiled more genuinely than she ever thought she could.

He blinked, studied her for a long moment, and then finally nodded. "Then they shall not be disappointed," he repeated and slowly escorted her down the stairs.

There were quiet gasps, murmurs, rumbles of conversations among the crowd. It wasn't until she and the king reached the last step that the crowd began to disperse, but the chattering, the speculation, and the gossip continued.

Calliope knew the men found themselves besotted by her beauty. Even so, only a small handful found their way to ask her onto the dance floor. As the night drew on, the celebration around her was in full swing despite the lack of coupling between the honored guest and her mate. She danced with her father and her sister's husbands more than any other.

"He will show." Hakan, the future king of Tolynn and Aithne's brother-in-law, assured her at one point. "Or you will show to him."

Confused, Calliope drew her eyebrows together, angled her head as Hakan led her in a slow twirl around another couple on the dance floor. "I do not understand."

"I had a similar conversation with Karan the evening of her celebration. As a matter of fact, I was dancing with her as I am with you now when she vanished from my arms and my sight."

Yes, Calliope remembered it well. Her sister's abrupt disappearance had created quite the uproar until their father managed, through his powers of divination, to see she had been transported to another world. A world where she found her mate, the incredibly delicious witch named Eric.

"The difference then and now," Hakan continued and spun her around again, "is that Karan was relieved no man present proved to be her chosen heart while you will be devastated if he does not show."

"He will be here." Calliope averted her gaze, not wishing for Hakan to see how truly worried she was that she could be wrong. What if he did not show? What if she waited her entire life for a night that would end like every other, alone, wanting, wishing?

Only a candle flicker of hope remained when she passed off Hakan to his wife with the fierce assurance she was fine. Dustin, Aithne's mate and captain of the guard of Tolynn, stepped in quickly to keep Calliope busy on the dance floor. She knew her family only wished to avert her attention from the obvious fact her mate's identity still remained unknown. Though it occurred to her once that her being in the arms of others all evening might deter her mate from approaching, she pushed the thought away. It was not how the customary joining worked. If he were present nothing and no one would stand between them. Aithne and Karan and even the queen already proved as much.

More than once as the night slowly drew to a close, as guests trickled out, their jaws flapping with speculation and opinions, Calliope felt as though someone watched her. The fine hairs at the nape of her neck stood on end, her skin prickled with awareness, and her belly quivered with the slightest of knowing sensations. But when she would turn, certain beyond her very being he was there, she would find nothing.

* * * *

He had not gone inside. Bronwen peered through the window of the grand ball room hidden by the deep shadows of night and watched her, wanted her, silently willed her to come to him even as he urged her to stay away. Reinn was right about everything. He could not have her. Even so, it did not change what was. He was meant to have her.

Bronwen watched as the man she danced with, a blond Fae he thought was named Dustin, stepped away, releasing Calliope from a companionable embrace. She smiled and that soft curve of shapely lips moved over Bronwen like a caress of silk. He had known she possessed a beauty so bright, so magnificent it blinded a man. Too bad for him that beauty fell short of lighting any darkness. She moved back from the Fae, cast a slow and searching glance around the room, disappointment, weariness, and confusion swirling in her cornflower eyes.

His arms ached with the absence of her trim body so fiercely it was as if he had been the one holding her, letting her go rather than Dustin. The low thrum of pain pumped through the blood he had taken in upon waking, scorching his body, tearing at his heart. He stepped aside, deeper into the shadows, needing a moment without her in his sights.

The shadows, he was always in the shadows, in the dark. How could he even think to have her with the curse laid upon him? How could he ever consider bringing her forever into the night?

"She is amazingly beautiful. A crisp slice of sunshine." Reinn's voice rang with an awe that surprised Bronwen. He had been sure his long time friend had been aware of Calliope's stunning physical appearance. Beneath the awe, Bronwen heard something more in the tone, something he could not pin.

"There is no other to rival her beauty," Bronwen said. He felt a hand on his back, a light comforting brush, and shot Reinn a look. He had perfect vision in the darkness, both did, and their gazes met in that quick instant, sensations and knowledge slicing between them like a double edged blade. Reinn's blondish-brown locks fell in haphazard curls around his square face, accenting perfect bone structure and wild electric green eyes. Eyes that so often portrayed the love he felt for Bronwen, love Bronwen so often ignored.

"To bring such beauty into our world would only kill it, kill her." Whatever had been in Reinn's tone was gone now, replaced by matter-of-factness that had Bronwen's temper flashing hot.

"Do you not think I know this? Do you not think I know the danger I would put her in?" Bronwen hissed the words, his head whipping to face Reinn. He ran his tongue over his teeth, felt the fangs starting to push through. Yes, definitely lit his temper flame with that one. It was that fact alone that held him back from claiming what was his. How could he strip such a woman from the light? He might be a monster, but even a monster could not be so cruel.

He leaned over, careful not to draw the attention of the few guests who remained inside the palace, some now gathered closer to the window. Calliope was surrounded by the king and queen, her sisters and their men. Her expression was troubled through she obviously tried to hide it with small smiles and feigned laughter. It was he she waited for, he who did not show. How could he leave her to wonder, to pine? How could he not? How could he walk away knowing the feelings inside him, the destiny meant to be shared?

His heart ached. A heart that had not beat in many millennia. Still, he could not bring himself to take what belonged to him, to take her from a world of light and happiness into one of darkness and gloom.

"Walk away, Bronwen." Reinn gently touched his arm. "We are not the only dangers of our world."

"No, but we shall protect her. If she comes to us, to me, we *will* protect her. It is the only way." Bronwen met Reinn's gaze and he saw the disapproval mixing with resignation in the other man's eyes. "The choice will be hers and hers alone. She will have until the dawn of next light to come to me."

* * * *

"I truly wish to be alone." Calliope entered her bedchamber with her sisters and her mother close at her heels. She might want nothing more than to be alone with her thoughts, her despair, but with the three women who loved her, she stood not a chance of getting that wish.

He had not showed. The celebration, the night she waited for her entire life came and went without a sign of her fated heart. Was loneness the real monster the curse upon her spoke of? A life doomed to darkness, alone for eternity, pining for love? For a woman such as she, there could be no greater death with no end than that.

"You do not need to be alone." Karan spoke firmly, an unmovable rock. She walked passed Calliope like a woman on a mission, her seething temper so thick around her even the sharpest of swords would have had trouble slicing through. "Let me find the son of a bitch. I will cut off his dick and feed it to him for breakfast for leaving you in the balance this way."

"Karan!" Her creative words and imagery had the queen and Aithne gasping in unison.

Despite her tattered heart and feelings, Calliope felt herself smile. It did not sound all that bad a punishment for the man so deemed to be her fated heart. Fitting for the embarrassment and pain he caused her this night.

"Sister is right." Aithne moved to Calliope's back, wrapped her arms around Calliope's waist, and rested her chin on her shoulder. Calliope thought she felt the baby in Aithne's stomach kick against her back, a light and comforting thump. "You should not be left alone when you are upset. You need your family now. You need us."

"I shall issue a declaration." The queen's tone was rigid, angered. "Your father will send out guards. We will find out who did not attend tonight's celebration. All in the lands were bid to come. Obviously, at least one did not."

Calliope looked to her mother, opened her mouth to speak and then, thinking better of it, closed her mouth again. It would likely do no good for any of them to point out how mere hours before the queen had been ready to defy her own law and cancel the celebration out of fear for who might show and turn out to be Calliope's destined heart. Instead, she closed her eyes and breathed deep. When she opened them again, her gaze landed on the bed, on the single red rose atop a scrap of parchment positioned on her pillow.

Her heart raced at the sight. It was from him, her mate, her destined. She need not look first to know. Twin arrows of fear and excitement speared through her as she slowly stepped out of Aithne's embrace and moved to the bed.

"What is it, Calliope?" Alarm rang with the curiosity in Karan's voice.

Calliope pretended not to hear her as she reached for the rose, the note beneath. The stem felt cool and stiff in her fingers. When she closed her hand around it to bring it to her nose for an indulgent sniff, she felt the prick of a thorn pierce her palm. She opened her hand and saw the small dab of blood. *An omen?* As she stared down at the words scrawled on the parchment and realized they were written in blood, she thought it must be.

"Calliope?" The same alarm echoed in Aithne's tone as she once again moved behind her and touched her shoulder.

"It is from him." There was no signature, no clue to his identity. The note gave only instructions of a place to go, and a deadline to be there. Still, everything in her being told her he had written the note. "He was here. He left this for me. I am to go to the top of the waterfall mountain before the sun rises on the next day and wait for him. Alone." She added the last word on a whispered breath of heightened fear tinged with anticipation. Emotions warred inside her, sensations she could not separate battling in her mind, her heart, between her legs.

The waterfall mountain. It was the highest point to the north of the goddess queen's lands. The peak was said to divide the light from the dark. The place where beyond turned into an Otherworld, which some even believed contained an Underworld. It would be a long journey of will, nerves, and expectation. A journey he wished her to make alone.

"You are not going." The queen's brisk, unarguable command had all the feelings accumulating inside Calliope crashing together, morphing into one. *Shock.*

"Mother, of course I will go." Clutching the note, the rose, she turned to face the queen.

"To the top of a mountain reputed to be a divider of Otherworld in the middle of the night to wait for a man you know not?" Aithne sounded horrified. "Sister, you cannot be serious!"

Though her answer was for Aithne, Calliope continued to gaze at her mother. "But I am serious."

"Then we will go with you." Karan stepped to Calliope's side.

Calliope felt the defiance, the aura of battle radiate from her sister. *Always ready to fight.* "No." She met Karan's hard edged insistence with a quieter, more certain tone of her own that was far more effective because of it. "I shall go alone as he bids."

"But the darkness, the monsters, the curse, you cannot—"

Calliope reached for Karan's hand even as she looked back at her mother. "It is my destiny. *He* is my destiny. Whatever I must face is meant to be."

The queen hesitated for so long Calliope was sure she would argue. Finally, her lips set in a grim line, eyes consumed with worry, she nodded. "Then you shall do as he bids."

Chapter Two

Dozens of stars scattered the pitch black sky, bringing about an ounce of light to a nearly moonless night. Only the smallest sliver of the moons visible in the goddess's lands could be seen as the phase began to wax from the new moon of the previous evening. There were no sounds save for the distant crashing of water into rock when Calliope topped the mountain flanked by her mother and father, her sisters and their husbands close at her backs. They insisted on accompanying her on her journey and she had to admit she was grateful in part. Karan's powers of projection allowed her to transport Eric, the king and queen, she had to make two trips as she could not move more than herself and one other at a time, to almost the exact point needed. As part winged Fae, Dustin had flown Aithne and Calliope, his arms tightly around them both as they soared through the night air. But the time for them to leave had come.

"It feels wrong to leave you here." Dustin ran his hands up and down her arms. His large wings created a golden backdrop for his muscular body, giving him a powerful image in the dark of the night. He flexed his wings, and flapped them lightly, stirring the air. "We can fly back as easily as we came. All you need to do is say the word."

"I cannot." She gazed into the Fae's eyes and saw understanding, a deep knowledge, and resignation. "It is right and I must do it alone. It is my destiny."

"So you have said many times." Dustin sighed and kissed her forehead. "Take care, little one." He stepped back and Karan and Eric moved in his place.

"Too bad there aren't any cell phone towers in your world." Eric pulled her into his strong arms and held her tight. "You would get a hell of a reception way up here."

"You can still call us if you find trouble." Karan closed in, too, hugging them both. "Eric will be watching, waiting."

"And at the first sign of trouble my lovely wife will poof us here and I'll burn the place down."

Calliope laughed and blinked back the sudden onset of tears. Eric was a witch from an otherworld with both the powers of vision and fire. Coupled with Karan's abilities of projection and natural personality to fight, they made quite a pair.

After a moment, Karan and Eric moved aside to stand with Dustin and Aithne, leaving the path open for the queen and king.

"I ask only once more." Her mother eyed her with seriousness and deep concern. "You are sure?"

"I am certain." Calliope put every ounce of conviction she felt into the words, letting none of the niggling fear show. "Go now, Mother, and do not worry for me."

"She blames herself for this." Her father said of her mother as Ina turned her back and moved out of earshot. "As do I."

"You did what you had to do. As am I."

Her father nodded and brushed his lips to her forehead much as Dustin had done. "Daria cursed our children to prevent you from ever ruling our lands, likely even to forever hold you in a blanket of unhappiness and fear. She underestimated the women you and your sisters would become."

With one last kiss, he too stepped away, leaving Calliope hoping beyond all else that he was right about the last. She watched them as they left her on the mountaintop. Karan and Eric vanished on the spot with the king and queen. Aithne flew away in the night sky safe in Dustin's arms.

Alone at last, Calliope turned and tried to ignore the rapidly increasing pace of her heart, the coolness spreading over her, moving through her that could only indicate a growing fear. She had managed to keep that particular emotion bottled inside, only dealing with a leak here and there since finding the summons from her mate last evening. Now, she felt the bottle shatter into a million pieces, the fear it contained seeping through every fiber of her being.

She had never cared to be alone, preferred instead to be surrounded by people, or at least, in the accompaniment of one or two others. Being the youngest of three daughters had made it relatively easy most her life. She had simply latched an invisible chain to her sisters. That chain was now snapped and she actually felt the loss of it, the freedom she did not want. It left her spiraling down a path without end or place to hold onto.

Legs shaking, she found a sturdy boulder near the pool of water at the start of the fall and sat. She focused on the sounds of the distant splash of water to rock at the mountain foot, lost herself in the rhythm rather than the fear that threatened to eat her alive, and started to sing while she waited for her man.

* * * *

The beauty of her voice rivaled that of her face. Bronwen watched her from afar, his eye sight as good and clear in the deep of night at great distances as any person or creature in the lands. His enhanced hearing worked well, too, and for a long time he simply listened. She sang a melody of softness and love that drifted to him on the air and caressed his skin like a physical touch. Now and then, a tear would glide down her lovely cheek and his heart would seize in his chest as if a fist squeezed at it, attempting to extinguish his artificial life.

She was frightened. How could she not be? Yet she had come to him as he had known she would. She waited for him. Again, as he had known she would. Her song continued to soothe the night air, slowly fading as the time passed until at last she curled on the boulder and drifted off to sleep.

With dawn quickly approaching, Bronwen went to her. He lifted her into his arms, careful not to wake her and then simply stood there holding her. Her slender body felt so delicate in his strong arms, like the rose he had left on her pillow at the palace of the goddess queen. She nuzzled her face against his chest, the heat of her even breaths warming his eternally cold flesh through the material of his shirt.

Bronwen closed his eyes and absorbed that heat, reveled in the sensation of it as it flowed through him. His gut was tight, quivering with desires and knowledge he realized so long ago and felt each and every time he had allowed himself a glimpse of her over the years. She stirred in her sleep, one arm moving around his back, the other slowly skimming up his chest to rest on his shoulder. His cock, never completely soft whenever he thought of her, saw her, grew hard and throbbing.

"It is you," she whispered, all statement and no question.

He opened his eyes and peered down at her. The breaths he need not take, but did anyway caught in his throat. But her eyes remained closed. "It is me, my love. Sleep now." He opened the power within him just a crack and pushed it over her, around her like a blanket to keep her in sleep.

She settled her head more comfortably against his chest and expelled a contented sigh. "I knew you would come. Not a monster. You are my true heart."

"Shhh." He heard himself make the sound, felt his lips come down to brush lightly over the top of her head. His mind, however, latched onto the words she mumbled in partial consciousness. Not a monster. Oh, yes, he was in quite possibly the worst sense of the word.

Bronwen knew of the curse upon her, knew more clearly than she that he *was* essentially the curse. Engulfed by a world of darkness. It was the spell. Thanks to his own curse, it was all he could offer her. To suffer a death with no end. *He* lived that death without end and, as he channeled his powers of flight to take Calliope home with him, he knew he could be sentencing her to much of the same.

* * * *

Calliope awoke groggy and disoriented. Her eyes opened slowly, her heart slamming into her throat when she found herself in a chamber she did not recognize, in a huge bed not her own. Sunlight, almost blindingly bright, streamed in through a part in the coverings over a ceiling to floor window, falling on rich wood, intricate carvings, and chiseled stone all draped or accented in some way by shimmering red silk. On the pillow beside her own lay a single red rose.

Her lips unfolded in a smile as she pushed herself up, and reached for the rose, remembering. He had come for her on the mountaintop in the night, brought her here, lain with her here in this bed. She could still feel the strength of his arms around her, the press of his hard body against her, and hear the gentle tone in his voice as he coaxed her back to sleep. Then he had lay with her, held her through what remained of the night, and protected her from the dark. She was not sure how she knew that, but she did. Now he was gone.

Carefully, as if sneaking out of bed beneath the watchful eyes of a guard, she got to her feet. She made no noise as she moved to a robe draped over the back of a nearby chair and shrugged it on over the nightdress she wore. A nightdress, she noted with a tickling sense of arousal, one that had not belonged to her before last night. One she had not been wearing when she had fallen asleep on the mountain.

He had changed her. He had removed her traveling clothing, dressed her in this lovely garment of red silk and fine lace. She caught her reflection in a mirror across the room and expelled a quiet gasp, her hand jerking up to cover her mouth. Her gaze traveled the length of her reflection. Not a nightdress, she thought in awe for a dress usually covered the body from hip to ankle. She took in the shortness of the gown, barely knee-length, the way the silk clung to her body, accenting her curves. She had never worn such revealing clothing and the sight only heightened the arousal, turning the tickle into a pulse.

She thought she looked like a very sexy sacrifice and found, to her sincere amazement and amusement, she minded not at all.

Her lips curved in a slight but decidedly devious smile. Before this moment, she would have thought the smile more suited to a face such as Karan's rather than her own. As the pulsing arousal hardened her nipples beneath the cool, fine material, coaxing warm juices between her pussy lips, she decided she liked seeing it on her own face.

A distant sound drew her attention to the door. Heart racing again, this time as much in anticipation as alarm, she forgot about the image in the mirror and went to the door. It creaked on its hinges as she pulled it open, the sound cutting through the tranquil air like a razor sharp dagger. She poked her head out first, leaning through the opening with only her upper body to peer around the frame down the semi-darkened hallway.

No windows. A very thin ray of light peeked from beneath a closed door farther down the hall on the opposite side. It was the only illumination to save the corridor from total blackness. Taking a deep breath for courage, she stepped out and made her way to that light.

Not a door, she realized when she finally neared it, but the start of a long, deep staircase. Hand gripping the rail as much for comfort as safety, she began the descent. Where were the windows? She saw none as she looked around, each step taking her down to an unknown destination amidst more semi-darkness, each step another test of sheer bravery.

She passed a candelabra on the wall, paused and squinted her eyes to examine it. The wicks of the candles had burned away long ago. An enormous chandelier of gorgeous crystal hung from the vaulted ceiling, the candles there barely visible as though burned to nubs and never replaced. She was halfway down before she saw the stairs made a sharp curve, halfway through the turn before she found it. Blessed light! Feeling equally foolish and elated, she sprinted down the remaining steps and saw him.

Her heart slammed against her breastbone even as she made a little squeak of surprise. Color rose to heat her cheeks and her hand flew up to cover her heart. "You scared me." She gave a shaky laugh that turned to a raspy breath as she settled her gaze on him.

Not the man from her every fantasy. She realized that in an instant. Yet, it was him. She had no doubt of that. Her belly quivered with a violent sensation so arousing and excitingly painful her hand slid from her heart to cover it. Flames erupted in her core, licking the inside of her channel, drawing out more of the juices she felt when looking in the mirror, until her pussy was sodden and aching with need.

He stood a head taller than her, his hair both blond and brown and many shades in between, the locks curly and left to fall haphazardly around his face and to his shoulders. Broad shoulders, she noted and remembered the feel of them beneath her hands. Her gaze skimmed to his arms, remembering them, too, as they carried her in her sleep. So strong, so comforting, so secure. A lean torso led to a slim waist and narrow hips all clad in black…black shirt, black breeches, black boots.

Wicked desires swam through her as she pulled her gaze back up. When her gaze met his, she felt herself drown in a sizzling ocean of electric green. Not the eyes she saw so often in her dreams either. These were brighter, colder, and harder.

"I awoke and you were not there." Her voice wobbled. Nerves, eagerness, arousal? Likely all of the above, she decided as he took a step toward her.

"I had things to do." Unlike her own, his voice was steady, brisk and as hard as his eyes. Eyes that slowly skimmed down her body in a leisurely appraisal that had her fighting not to squirm even as a trickle of wetness slid down her inner thigh.

"I missed you." Something flickered over his face at that, a quick flash that happened so fast she might have imagined it. He continued to advance on her, his eyes darkening with intent and desire. Her breathing became ragged and her pulse pounded in her ears, but neither could be attributed to fear. This man was her mate, her heart, and if that expression in his eyes were any indication at all, he fully intended to claim her as such right here in the foyer.

* * * *

Reinn knew he should back away, knew he shouldn't touch her. He stalked toward her slowly as he would in his wolf form easing onto prey. His gut was a jumble of hunger and nerves, needs and battles he stood no chance of winning. He'd realized it while standing with Bronwen outside the goddess queen's palace. The moment he spotted Calliope through the window he had known. He was her intended, her true heart, her mate.

He had wanted to run then, to flee back to this castle in the underworld and lick his wounded heart, his pride until both were numb and dormant. How could it be? How could she be meant for Reinn when Bronwen was so certain *he* was her destined? How could she be meant for Reinn when Bronwen was the one Reinn wanted? But as Reinn gazed at her now, his eyes drinking in every inch of her delicious body clad in that dick-teasing red silk pitiful excuse for a nightdress, he knew he wanted her, *needed* her, too.

And where had this vixen come from? Was Calliope not the most beautiful of the three daughters born to the goddess queen? The fragile daughter? The innocent and most sweetly feminine of the three? Standing before him with her tumble of sunny blond hair mussed, cheeks slightly flushed, and an expression on her face that was both daring and teasing behind the trepidation, wearing clothing that barely covered her smoothly tanned flesh, she appeared anything but innocent and frail.

His cock throbbed in the confines of his breeches. His hands ached to touch. His mouth watered with the desire to taste, to explore, to feed. Tamping down the last urge now was not the time to allow the beast inside him free reign, he dragged his gaze from her shapely legs to her face. The dark desire brightened only by a hint of fear in her cornflower eyes was his undoing.

Reinn circled her, his senses on high alert as he fed on her scent, sweet and floral and frightened. He heard her breaths, ragged and uneven, saw the slightest shiver of her body as his aura invaded hers.

Calliope didn't turn to face him, but stood statue still as he moved around her. Only when he stopped in front of her, attempting to close the distance between their bodies, did she step back. It was an involuntary step, a reflex action, he knew, but it fueled the predatory desires inside him.

She gazed at him searchingly, head tilted back to meet his eyes, the smooth line of her neck exposed. He would save that tantalizing flesh for Bronwen, but the rest he intended to sample now.

"You forgot to tie the robe." He pushed a hand under one side of the silky material, curled his fingers around her slim waist, and felt the tremble of her body all the way to his toes. "Why bother to put it on if you are going to leave on display what is underneath?"

"I..." She gulped, licked her lips, and his attention was instantly there.

The shape of her mouth reminded him of a heart-shaped bow in a glistening pale pink. His dick flexed at the thought of feeling the moisture her tongue left behind on his shaft, of having that tongue glide up and down his length as smoothly as it slid over her bottom lip.

"Did you wish me to explore what is beneath?" He pushed his hand up, framing her side with his palm, reveling in the continued tremor of her body beneath his touch.

"I..." She began again, gasping abruptly when he caught her waist in his other hand and yanked her hard against him.

Her body molded to his, her gentle curves conforming to the hard planes of his chest as though they were a perfect fit. He felt her heart beating rapidly and intense, and could smell her blood now, pumping viciously in her veins. He smelled her essence, too, faintly sweet and heavy in the air around them. The beast inside him stirred.

"You are mine now." He all but growled the words, heard the utter possession in the roughness of his tone. He couldn't stop it, couldn't ignore the truth of it.

"Yes." The word spilled from her delectable mouth on a whispered gasp, the corners of her lips twitching ever so slightly in a pleased smile. "I am yours. Always."

The declaration pierced through the wildness in his mind, slapped at the beast within him, and caused his head to jerk back. She should be saying those words to Bronwen. How would he feel when he discovered she was not for him after all, but for Reinn? How would he react when he discovered Reinn had been with her this day while Bronwen slept the sleep of the dead in his room below ground?

A low, rumbling sound tore through his throat. Not quite the growl of his wolf but far more animalistic than any man. Her eyes widened and her body stilled in his arms. He wanted to tell her not to be afraid of him, but that was exactly what she should be. She should fear him. Right now he feared himself. He felt torn, between the love of a man he had been with for more millennia than she had lived and the love of a woman bound to him by destiny.

"Take me if you wish." She touched his face, her palm cupping his cheek. Her hand shook but only a little. "Explore my body for it is yours now."

Reinn felt the last string on his resistance snap. With another tormented growl, he covered her breast with one hand, wrenching the robe from her body with the other. The low, throaty sounds she made caressed the beast within him and awakened more hunger than he ever thought to feed.

* * * *

It was like being ravished by a wild animal let loose from a cage. If this was the type of monster the spell spoke of, Calliope thought she would thank dear Daria after all. His hand on her breast squeezed, kneaded, and her head fell back, eyes closing from the pleasure of having a man's hands, *her* man's hands on her body. Her arms folded around his neck, fingers lacing in the hairs at his nape. His breath was warm, a heated caress that teased and tormented the sensitive line of her jaw. She moaned, both in pleasure and encouragement when he nipped and licked his way to her mouth and then, *thank the guardians*, his lips closed over hers.

His tongue pushed its way into her mouth not waiting for invitation. It took as he took, tangling with hers in a dance as old as time, adding a recklessness that brought the thrill and torture to an all new high. Her pussy flamed, aching with a desperate need to be touched, entered, and ravished. Her nipples throbbed, hardening past the point of pain in their mirroring need for satisfaction.

"Please." She heard the word, heard the whispered plea in it, but did not realize at first it came from her own lips. He licked his way over her cheek, her jaw, her throat, and danced a fiery line along the heart-shaped bodice of the nightdress, as she writhed in his arms.

His hand on her waist fisted in the nightdress, holding her lower body so firmly against him she felt the evidence of his erection hard and long against her belly. Pinpoints of sizzling rapture tore through her as the hand on her breast released, gripped the thin silk of the nightdress and together with the hand at her waist, shredded it from her body. Then he was delving between her legs, one hand pushing through the vee of her thighs to cup her sodden sex.

By the guardians! The feel of his roughened hand to her sensitive intimate flesh drove her mindless with longing and needs. Her hips rotated, her pussy grinding into his palm, her breasts pressed against his chest, nipples beading and screaming for attention.

He plunged inside her weeping channel. Two fingers, maybe three, thrust into her without preparation or warning. He threw his head back and howled. "Gods! Sweet Gods! So wet, so hot, so tight." His fingers probed her tender opening, a vicious, rapidly moving piston that stretched her channel and stroked her core to scalding ecstasy.

She needed to touch, to feel his flesh. It was the one clear thought that made it through the sexual fog in her mind. Her hands grabbed at his shoulders, fingers scratching, nails biting in her attempts to free him of the shirt covering him. She managed to find leverage in the collar and yanked, reveling in the sound of ripping material. Then she felt the smoothness of flesh, the rigidness of muscle beneath her hands.

He seemed to fold himself over her, his tongue tracing its way down the valley between her breasts, and then his mouth closed over one nipple. Exquisite pleasure rocketed through her as he sucked her breast between his lips, his tongue lapping over her beaded, throbbing nipple, his teeth closing around the taut peak. When he bit her nipple, her hips bucked, driving his fingers deeper still inside her and the orgasm, barely hanging on by a stroke, tore from her on a wail of sounds and lights and sensations.

Her nails dug into the skin of his shoulders as her body convulsed with the release and still, he continued to ram his fingers inside her pulsing channel, continued to bite and roll her nipple between his teeth. Dimly, she felt his other hand move between them, only half consciously registering the feel of his hand as it fumbled with the ties of his breeches.

Too soon, she thought, but could not find the strength to say the words. He meant to take her now, to shove his hard cock in her pussy and it was too soon. Her muscles still shuddered from the orgasm, the tender flesh of her channel afire from the continued assault of his fingers. Her legs trembled and only his lightning fast hands kept her from slinking to the floor. He pulled his fingers from her pussy, both arms moving to her hips and then he was lifting her into his arms.

"Wrap your legs around my waist." The order came in a gruff, almost beastly tone. "Take me inside you. I will have my cock inside you while the orgasm still quakes within you."

Too soon, she thought again, but even as the words flittered through her mind, her legs were closing around his waist, ankles locking in place behind his back. The position rammed his cock inside her with little more finesse than he had done with his fingers before. In one violent pump of his hips, one vicious yank of his hands on her bottom, he slammed his cock in balls deep inside her and had them both screaming from the sharp pain, the splendid pleasure.

He carried her, backing her against a nearby wall, and held her there while he pumped his cock in and out of her pussy in brisk, measured thrusts. "Yes! So tight. I can feel it, the way your body still jerks with the orgasm I gave you. The way you're squeezed around my dick."

She felt it too and so much more. His hands gripped her ass, the tips of his fingers bruising as he held her in place, pinned her to the wall, and pounded his cock in her channel. Each thrust was a test in both control and resiliency. Each long slide out caused her pussy to weep from the retreat. Each hard ram in had her breath catching and her voice screaming. His cock filled her to the point of bursting, so long and thick she thought it possible to split her in two. And the low rumbling growls he made as he pounded in her sensitive channel brought her a sense of intense satisfaction she never thought to know.

Her nails raked his shoulders and his back beneath the tattered material of his shirt. He sucked a breath through his teeth, his head coming up. His gaze met hers for the first time since he began to take what he wanted from her, since he began to explore her body as she bid him.

His eyes were no longer the sensational green, but a deep green so dark it was nearly black. The expression in them struck her as so primal, so domineering that it brought a little trickle of the fear back to the surface of her senses. Fear she rode on as ferociously as he rode her body.

"You are marking me." He sounded both surprised and pleased by the fact. Sweat slid in rivulets down his handsome face, his neck, created a sheen of slickness over his shoulders and back.

"H—how?" She did not understand. Was it not he who held her? He who controlled her?

"Your nails are digging into my flesh."

"I am sorry. Did I hurt you?"

A faint smile tilted his lips. "No. I like it. Continue and I shall do the same for you next time."

She was not so certain she would enjoy his nails scraping at her flesh like knives, but before she could tell him so, he pulled back until only the head of his cock remained in her pussy, then gaze locked with hers, thrust into her so hard and fast that thought became a thing of the past. Her nails buried in his flesh and she knew she drew blood, but could not loosen her grip as the onslaught of another orgasm stole her restrain.

"Come for me, Calliope." He growled the words, his face contorting in pleasure and pain, domination and satisfaction. "Come for me now!" He crushed his mouth to hers, ravaged her mouth as he did her body, and she had no hope of stopping the orgasm. She cried out her release into his mouth, nails biting, hips pumping, body thrashing as he too found the explosive end of his control.

Not until the last drop of fluids released between them did he stop his thrusts, and slowly lower her to lean against the wall. Her legs wobbled, heart pounding so rapidly she feared heart failure, breaths too rapid to offer enough oxygen.

He held himself up, hands resting on the wall on either side of her head, eyes closed as he fought his body to breathe, to stand, to calm. Unable to move, she simply stared at him, emotions flowing through her so many and varied she dared not attempt to define them. After a long moment, his eyes opened. The electric green was back with something new in their depths, something that was not quite anger, not quite fear or regret, but somewhere in between the three.

He stared at her then, as if reaching some sort of decision in his mind, straightened, moved to pick up her robe, and thrust it at her. "Go back to your chamber. Change." He did not look at her but busied himself with the retying of his breeches. "There will be food in the dining room when you return."

Before she could find words to say, he turned and left her breathing heavily, stark naked, body humming from the delicious abuse of his hands, mouth, and cock against the foyer wall.

Chapter Three

Calliope found the dining room deserted, the long rectangular table set for one at the end closest the door. Light flooded the room through the opened drapes of the large windows displaying dust likely more than an inch thick on every surface but the table. She guessed the room did not get much use. Even so, in a castle this size, did the man not have servants to clean, to cook, to tend?

"Hello?" The word spilled quietly from her lips, but in the silence of the enormous decidedly empty room, it sounded like a siren's wail. She turned where she stood just inside the doorway and saw only more unoccupied room behind her. When her gaze landed on the section of the wall where she had been so masterfully taken to a delicious abyss not long before, her belly grumbled in hunger even as delighted sensations tingled through her mind and core.

Smiling ever so slightly, she turned back to the dining room, to the table, and saw the rose. It was white this time. A single white bud that had barely begun to bloom when plucked from its branch. Beneath it lay a note: *Eat your fill, my love, and roam free in the castle this day. I will return to you soon, Reinn.*

Not written in blood this time, she noted as she studied the parchment, her gaze centering on the name. Reinn. Guardians, she had not realized she failed to even find out his name before now. He had swept her off her feet as she always dreamed, brought her to this lovely, if a bit unkempt, castle, showed her delights in the way of the flesh she had not known, and she had not even bothered to learn his name.

She laughed, happiness and enjoyment rippling through her in waves as she sat before the meal he left for her. Perhaps he was not the dark haired, dark eyed stranger from her every fantasy, but Reinn with his blondish-brown curls and rock-hard body was definitely so much more.

As she ate her fill, her eyes scanned the room. She had not seen nor heard any servants in her time since waking. Given that Reinn had not seemed unabashed to engage in intimacies in the open foyer where anyone could have seen, she gathered if there were servants on the premises, they did not stay within the main castle.

Servants or not, the rooms needed a woman's touch, she decided as she finished her meal and rose to peruse her new home. The furnishings were sparse and all of dark woods and hard stone. Drapes and fabrics were both colored in black or red and drowned out much of the light that managed to peek in through the large windows in the chambers. Though beautiful, the castle was too dark, too stuffy, and far too masculine.

In a palace of servants, guards, and keepers, she had never cleaned a day in her life. Still, Calliope did not see such a thing as beneath her. Humming softly, she set about removing dust, restoring color and light, and adding her own personal touches to her new home.

* * * *

Bronwen had not known the dead could dream. For the first time in centuries, the animated visions of color and substance came to him in the form of Calliope as he slept. When he awoke, it was to the sound of her voice once again carrying to him on the air. This time the sweet melody was more upbeat, energetic, and happy. She was happy. The realization brought him both a sense of relieved elation and tense trepidation.

He followed the sounds of her song and found her before the mirror in the chamber he had deemed hers. In the shadows of the doorway, he watched her as she pushed a brush through her satiny strands, his palms itching to feel as the hairs fell in a flowing curtain around her slim shoulders. He reveled in her scent, her voice, her presence. After a time, he shifted, leaned a shoulder against the doorframe, and her song skipped a beat. In that moment, she knew he was there. Still, she did not turn, did not stop singing until she finished the song. Something Celtic, he deduced, about a goddess of love and her chosen mate. Fitting, he mused, given the circumstances.

In the darkness of a new night, his worry for her wellbeing, his regret of what must be, sank beneath the love in his heart and the desires of his body for her. His gut quivered with the fierce needs to be near her, his cock aching to be inside her, to claim her. His mind reeled with the myriad of ways he wished to be with her tonight and every night hereafter.

When she put down the brush on the table before her, her hand sliding down to cover her belly, he knew she felt the same quiver as he. A smile unfolded on his lips even as the tremor spread to his heart, his loins. Never had he seen a woman so beautiful. Never had the agony to touch been so great.

"You came back." Her soft words pulled him from his trance. "I wondered when you would. Why did you stay away so long?"

He could not tell her. Not yet. The daughter of the goddess queen mated to a monster for all eternity, it was still too much for even his mind to grasp. So delicate, so lovely, so tenderly sweet and fragile, paired with a creature of the night, of blood and darkness such as himself. He would have her comfortable with him first, marked as his beyond destiny but in true heart and body. Then perhaps he would tell her the truth. Then perhaps he could reveal that he was a vampire.

"I had business." He did not move from his position leaning against the doorframe, feared he might stumble if he tried. She turned, her long hair draped over her shoulders and falling over her breasts like blond ribbons. She wore no clothes, he realized, surprise racing through him even as his dick leapt to instant attention. The blood he had consumed only moments before pumped wildly through his veins as his gaze landed on large rosy brown taut nipples peeking through the satiny strands.

"The castle, it is a beautiful home, so many chambers to explore."

He stiffened. Reinn should have kept watch on her. Had he allowed her to roam free? What if she had come across Bronwen's chamber beneath the stairs? What if she had come across his cold, lifeless body?

"I am pleased that you like it as it is your home now."

She smiled, a sensual tilt of her lips that had his dick throbbing in jubilation and eagerness. "Yes, it is my home now." She angled her head, the smile turning just a bit devious. He had not expected to see such a look on her face and the sight sent his senses on a whirlwind of possibilities. "Are you going to come inside? Or do you wish to stand in the door all night?"

He chuckled to himself and shook his head. "It seems I have underestimated you. Your boldness surprises me, little one, as does your state of undress. Not that I mind." He let the smile on his face sound in his voice as he straightened from the doorframe and took a small step into the room.

She shrugged. "I thought it would save you the trouble of ripping my clothes from my body."

Bronwen's balls gave a ferocious jerk in his breeches that had his step faltering and his heart doing a slow and very delicious roll in his chest. Demons save him, the woman was magnificent! "And would you trouble to do so for me this night?"

"If my strength does not fail me, I would." She shook her hair behind her shoulders as she got to her feet and faced him.

Her body was a tribute to all that was godly. Smooth lines and generous curves, perfect angles and delectable points. He might have wished the opportunity to peel clothing from her body, to experience the change beneath his palms of cool material to warm downy flesh.

Next time, he promised himself as he took another step forward. For how could he argue with a woman so obviously naked and willing?

"Do you anticipate my touch to drain your strength, little one? Does your control grow weak in my presence?" He hoped so. Oh, how he longed to make her lose all control of muscles, of heart, of self. His gaze traveled down her body as he moved into the flickering light of the candles, his mind already planning exactly the ways he intended to accomplish his goal. His mouth watered, went dry and then watered again as he pictured himself licking his way up her body, stopping for long moments to savor the taste of her sweet essence. When his fangs began to extend he forced his gaze away from the tempting treat of her inner thigh, moved his attention up to her slightly rounded belly, her abdomen, the enticing mounds of her breasts.

"It does. Though I do believe I am not alone in that response."

"Little one, you are so right." Control would be battle of wills between them. It was something he never expected of her, yet he found it to be a pleasant surprise. His cock revved for the challenge, the blood in his veins moving from simmering to boiling from the sheer heat she was building inside him. He could not remember ever feeling so warm, so ready, and so alive. Not in all the centuries since the vampire curse took him under. "I wonder which of us shall lose the battle first. I fear it might be me."

He observed her satisfied smile as he drew his gaze up to meet hers, watched as that smile slowly faded as he came fully into the light. He saw when the change came over her though he knew not the cause. Her incredible eyes widened, her breath hitched, her body stiffened. A wave of fear washed over her in a palpable rush before it shattered to a mist of confusion and wonder. It brought his masculine senses to high alert even as the vampire he was fed on the anxiety and sudden nerves.

"It is you." Her words sounded of both statement and question, of recognition and wonderment. Her shoulders trembled as a ragged breath pushed from her lungs. "I do not understand."

Bronwen narrowed his eyes. Something about her response did not seem right. What did she not understand? He knew he should ask, but the growing need inside him, the hunger tearing its way through his gut overtook his sensibility. So close to her now, he could not think, only feel and consume.

"I have waited for you more years than you could know." He wanted to touch her, but resisted the urge, reveling in the anticipation for a moment longer. It drove him mad, her intoxicating scent of pure woman and heavy arousal, the sound of her heart racing rhythmically and strong in her chest, the scent of her blood as it pumped through her veins. If he touched her now with so many of his senses, both vampire and man, on-line as they were, he feared he might harm her. It was the last thing he wished to ever do.

She stood ramrod still as he moved behind her and only then did he allow himself to feel. He pushed her hair to the side, watching in abstract fascination as her head arched into the touch exposing the long, slender line of her neck. He could not stop himself. He leaned in, buried his face in her neck, breathed in the warmth of her flesh, the floral undertones, felt the pulse beneath his closed lips. His fangs extended, sharp pinpoints that cut into his lower lip and drew blood.

Bronwen jerked his head back, turned from what would surely be his most delicious meal ever, and closed his eyes. Control. He had been right to believe he would be the first to lose it. He could not lose it with her. He would not take her in that way, would not turn her, no matter the temptation.

* * * *

Calliope's mind whirled even as her body gave a visceral reaction to his closeness, his touch. This was the man from her dreams, the man she thought always to be her destined heart, her true mate. She felt it so thoroughly in her bones that mistaking the signs could not be an option. Yet how could that be? Had she not felt the same bone-deep response to Reinn?

She felt his body jerk behind her and knew he looked away. His fingers held her hair away from her neck, the chill of them against her warm nape a contrast that had her fighting off a shiver. *So cold.* Why was his hand so incredibly icy?

Wishing to warm him for reasons she could not define, could not understand, she reached behind her, found his other hand at his side and brought it around her waist, holding it over her belly. It, too, was freezing. She tilted her head back, looked over her shoulder and found the pale line of his neck in her vision. Daringly, she leaned in, rising to her toes as she licked from the bend of his shoulder to the smooth patch of flesh behind his ear. He shuddered, so violently she felt it against her back though there remained a full inch of space between their bodies.

It was invigorating, to draw such response from a man. Nerves warred with needs, confusion with senses, and reality with dreams. Where was Reinn? Who was Reinn? She could not think on that now, could not focus. Instead, she marveled in the feel she recognized always, the feel she had mistaken for Reinn, but found now with this man. This man. She would not give herself to another again without first learning his name.

"What am I to call you?" Her soft words split the tension, both sexual and intangible, in the room like a double edged sword. His head slowly turned, his gaze falling upon hers and the sight of those dark as pitch eyes from her dreams pushed their way into her reality with a jolt of feminine juices through her very core. "I have waited to see those eyes on me for more years than you could know." She did not mean to say it aloud, did not realize she did until those eyes softened, and glimmered with a pinkish watery mist.

"Bronwen." His voice hitched on the name. "I am Bronwen. And you are everything my heart has ever needed, in warmth and cold, in light and darkness." He released her hair, his hand coming to her cheek as his lips closed in on hers.

The kiss was nothing like those she shared with Reinn. Softer, sweeter, more tender. He licked the outside of her lips, urging them to part, and then delved inside with a patient and hesitant way that had her breathless and moaning into his mouth.

She turned slowly in his arms, needing to be face to face, to feel his body long and hard against hers. He was taller than Reinn, but seemed to judge their difference in height easily, and bent his knees to accommodate her, folding himself around her, one hand continuing to cup her cheek, the other holding her securely though gently around her waist.

Every move he made spoke of tenderness and devotion, of a need to please and a fear of harming. She felt like a prized possession in his arms, delicate and unsullied, desired and delightful. It was such a contrast to the way Reinn had taken her earlier that day, a calm reprieve after a turbulent storm. She had taken pleasure in the storm, thrived on the roughness and submitting of power. She would now enjoy the serene, and get gratification from the surrendering of body and self.

She reached between their bodies, the need to feel his flesh against hers so overpowering now that her hands shook as she fought to pull his shirt free of the waistband of his breeches. Her hands delved beneath the material, cascading up the rigid plane of his stomach, the sharp bumps of his abs, the rippling muscles of his chest. So cold, her mind registered again, all so icy beneath the warmth of her palms.

His mouth moved from hers, tongue licking, teeth grazing along her cheek, her neck. The shiver moved through her, the expectancy of a quick nip, the awareness he would do no more than tease. Her hands turned beneath his shirt and fisted, but she could not tear the fabric.

She growled, a sound she never heard from her own throat, and heard him chuckle albeit breathlessly against her neck.

"Were you right after all, little one? Has your strength deserted you?"

"Completely. *Please*, I wish to feel you. I want my hands on you." She tugged at the shirt, almost mindless now in her need to see him, to fully touch him. "You are so cold. Let me warm you."

Something moved through his eyes as he leaned back, something akin to sorrow or regret. He reached for the hem of his shirt, yanked it over his head, and tossed it to the floor. He gave his head a shake, his black hair sleek and shimmering in the candlelight falling like an opulent curtain behind his broad shoulders. When his gaze met hers again, whatever she had seen was gone, replaced once more by heat and sheer longing.

She felt mirroring emotions flood her own eyes as she feasted on the pale flesh now bared for her gaze. Her hands trembled slightly as she splayed them on his chest, rubbed them through the patch of ebony hairs that covered his pecs. Mouth watering, she leaned in and traced the outline of those pecs with the tip of her tongue. When she heard the low purr of sound he made, she looked up at him from under her lashes and saw him fling his head back, his own eyes closed, his expression one of pure rapture.

"Calliope, ah, little one, your tongue is like a flame to my skin." His whispered groans drifted over her, seeped into her, tightening her nipples and drawing at the juices flowing in her core.

More, was all she could think. She wanted to warm more of his chilled flesh, to taste more of him on her tongue. She bent her knees, and started to lick her way down his torso, but he caught her in his arms and lifted her. Refusing to be deterred, she let her arm slide around his back, her other hand braced on his chest as she returned to his pecs, alternating a lick for a kiss for a gentle rasp of teeth.

He carried her to the bed, laying her down as tenderly as he would a delicate rosebud, going down with her to cover her with his half naked body, his lips finding hers. The press of his lower body to her center was a marvelous pressure and she wrapped her legs around his waist, brought her bare pussy to grind against the chilly leather of his breeches and the rock hard cock they concealed.

The kiss became ravenous, somewhere between a mild tasting and a wild taking, as his hands framed her sides, glided down to her hips, and gripped. Then his mouth was moving from hers to trail those icy-fevered kisses down her chin, pausing to do deliciously disturbing things to her throat, before moving on to her collarbone, and finally her breasts.

"Bronwen! Ah Gods." She cried out as he tugged one nipple between his lips, rolled it, suckled it, and teased it with his tongue. The torment ended far too soon as he released her nipple and trailed the tip of his tongue down the crevice over her abdomen. He stopped at her bellybutton, traced the outer rim, did a quick dive inside that had her laughing albeit breathlessly, and then continued down.

She trembled and expelled a quiet moan when his kisses and licks led him to the apex of her middle. But rather than linger as she expected, rather than traveling further to the excruciating throb in her pussy, he veered down her right thigh. He sampled a path over her knee, her shin, her ankle, his body all the while gliding down the bed and off, his hands skimming in their descent.

He stood, gaze transfixed on her body, and untied his breeches, slowly peeled them off. The expression in his eyes was so hot, so primordial that she felt her sensory nerves spike beyond natural feel. Power coasted over her, seeped into her, even as more poured out of her in waves. Girl power, Karan would have called it and Calliope experienced it now, seeing the effect she had on the man looking down at her.

The power was met with an opposing force. She could almost hear it crackle in the air between them as she stared at Bronwen, exploring every glorious inch of him she could see with her gaze. She would not have been able to take her eyes off of him if she had wished to. His long, pale legs with wide, strong thighs led to a cock of exquisite male perfection. It lay against his body, impossibly wide, gloriously long and so obviously luscious and hard. Though she knew she should look further, she could not seem to push her gaze beyond the part of him her body yearned to have most.

"Wow!" The word rolled out of her mouth before she could think to prevent it. She had not been given the chance to visually examine Reinn this way, only to feel. That had been beyond superb and in comparison—she knew she really should not compare the two men but how did a woman dare not?—the anticipated feel of the seemingly wider and longer Bronwen had her pussy convulsing in equal apprehension and enthusiasm.

Bronwen flexed that impressive part of him and she whipped her gaze up to meet his, felt her cheeks heat at the embarrassment of being caught staring at his cock. His lips, a lovely blood red with a perfect point in the center of the upper one, were tilted in a very knowing, amused and wickedly sexy grin.

"Do not be embarrassed, little one. I like that you look at me that way." He reached for her leg, his hands framing her shin and stroking down to her ankle as he lifted it. Gaze always locked with hers, he drew her big toe into his mouth, sucked, nibbled, tickled. How that one move, that one insignificant part of her body could be so erotic, so erogenous, she could not say, even if she had been able to find a steady breath for words.

He released her toe, his mouth moving to alternate a sizzling kiss, a teasing lick, a tickling brush of teeth to her instep, her heel, her ankle until he was traveling back up her body on a decided course to the one spot she wanted that mouth most.

He paused when he reached her inner thigh, his tongue dancing along her heated flesh. He sucked her skin between his lips and rolled it as he had done with her nipple. She squirmed, the act pulling tiny whimpers from her throat.

Something sharp grazed over that skin, a spiky point that had an arrow of eager alarm barreling through her. Her vision went red. In that one instant, she saw a haze of murky red, tasted something faintly coppery on her tongue, and a decided chill brought goose pimples to her flesh.

Bronwen wrenched his head back, his eyes closed, his mouth agape and glistening with the moisture of her juices leaking from her drenched sex. He shivered between her thighs before diving once more. His mouth covered her pussy, closing around her feminine lips. His tongue thrust inside her channel and the red turned to a white-hot rapture of sensation that had her head lolling and her mind lost in the wonder.

Her fingers fisted, released, and fisted again when she buried them in his hair. His tongue worked her slowly, gradual plunges into her channel, smooth retreats that sizzled and burned. She held him to her pussy, her hands unmovable on his head, as her body writhed and rode the sweet edge of power and building pressure.

Faster. More. The tenderness in which he consumed her essence tormented her to a point of sheer agony bordering on the most overwhelming pleasure, pleasure that remained frustratingly just out of reach.

"Please." She forced herself to release her hold on his hair, her arms coming up to grip at the pillow on either side of her head. Mistake, she realized in an instant. With his ability to move restored, his tongue recoiled, his lips sliding over her clit before he began his slow, titillating climb once more up her body. When he reached her breasts, he lingered, teasing, nipping, sucking, and drawing panting moans and breathy pleas from her lips. "Bronwen!"

His head came up, his face a mixture of torment of his own desires and sheer masculine satisfaction of what he did to her. He shifted, lined his body with hers and the pressure of his weight, of each muscular ridge and smooth contour, brought her to a new level of ecstasy.

"Your lip is bleeding." And the sight of that tiny drop of red on his lower lip sent a ripple of thrilled panic coursing to her toes. She slid her arms around his neck, pulled his face down to meet hers, and licked that droplet away. When she looked into his eyes, what she saw there had her heart tripping, flipping and racing all in succinct succession. Carnal lust, power, iniquitous torture swirled in indescribable colors in the deepest depths of the black.

"Why did you do that?" His voice was harsh, rough.

She shrugged. "Impulse."

"You are so much more than I ever expected, little one." He kissed her jaw, shifted his hips more comfortably between her spread thighs. "The taste of you is more enchanting than a dozen stars, the feel of your flesh softer than a cloud." His cock nudged at the outer edge of her pussy, not entering but teasing, tormenting. "I will take you now. Are you ready to feel me inside you?"

"Yes." She said the word on a breathless plea as she nipped his bottom lip and caught another trickle of blood with her tongue. The coppery taste mixed with the remnants of her juices on his flesh and she groaned in appreciation of her own flavor, of his. "Yes!" She groaned again as he eased the head of his cock into her opening.

"You are so tight, little one, so wet." He ground the words through gritted teeth, pushing his dick gently inside her, stretching her, filling her.

Her hands were in his hair again, fingers lacing through the velvety strands, fisting as her pussy expanded to accommodate his width. "Gods, Bronwen!"

She wanted to lift her hips, to drive his cock balls deep inside her in one vicious thrust of pain-laced pleasure rather than allowing him to continue to torture her this way. The slow technique he used to sheath his cock with her pussy walls left her incensed and teetering on the edge of sanity even as the orgasm mounted to rally for speed and release against the prolonged intrusion.

"I have waited for this moment far too long. To think I nearly denied myself this pleasure."

She would be damned if she would allow him to deny either of them this pleasure. Calliope dug her heels into the bed, used it for leverage to lift her hips, and arched her head back when his cock at last slid deeply home. The sounds they both made, grunts, groans, entwined to become one as they set a pace together that was equally deliberate and amazing, ravenous and gratifying.

"Calliope, ah, little one." The words sounded wrenched from his throat. She felt him fighting to keep control, to keep the measured pace he set.

"Mmm, let yourself go, Bronwen. It is your turn to go weak at my touch." And to make sure he did, she released her grip on his hair, reached between their bodies and curled her thumb and forefinger around the half-inch of his shaft that was not buried inside her channel and squeezed.

Bronwen braced his hands on either side of her shoulders, threw his head back, and thrust stiff and deep, long and measured strokes that remained as slow and steady as before but hit harder and farther with each inward plunge. The fingers around his shaft rubbed against her clit as their bodies came together. The combination had her screaming from the euphoric release of her body and mind. Dimly she heard him reach his own fulfillment and somewhere in the distance a wolf howled in the night.

* * * *

"Will you be here with me tomorrow?" Calliope's voice was sleepy, soft in the serene atmosphere that had fallen over the bedchamber. "Will you spend the day with me as well as the night?"

She lay in the crook of his arm, her cheek resting on his chest, fingers idly twiddling with the patch of dark curls that scattered on his pecs. Bronwen could feel her heart against his ribs, the slow and rhythmic beat both a comfort and a torment after the love they shared, the question left to dangle in the silence.

"No." She deserved an explanation, but he could not think of one that would even remotely be true and he hated the lies between them, hated that he had to keep so much from her in his quest to both have and protect.

She sighed. Bronwen closed his eyes and reveled in the feel of her warm breath gliding over his chilled skin. As always, it was both arousing and pure torture. He should have no right to take that warmth from her. Yet he knew destiny had given him exactly that right. What made the guardians so cruel as to form such a paring, to couple two hearts cursed as they both were?

"I suppose I shall occupy myself with the second floor tomorrow then."

Pulled from his thoughts by confusion, Bronwen angled his head to look at her. "Occupy yourself how on the second floor?"

She giggled, the sound girlish and playful. "Well, since you shall not be up here to offer distraction, I was thinking I would continue my cleaning in these chambers."

"Cleaning?" he repeated dumbly.

She lifted her head, rested her chin on his chest and gazed up at him beneath long, sultry lashes. "Yes, cleaning. Do you not have servants to care for this place?"

Bronwen felt the sudden and totally uncharacteristic urge to squirm. "There is Reinn. He is all who resides here besides me."

She stiffened at the name. If he had not been holding her so close, looking directly at her, he might not have noticed.

"Well, he does not do a good job at keeping the castle fit to live." She frowned, settled her head back on his chest, and sighed again. "I suppose that is what happens when two men are left to live alone."

Bronwen chuckled at the dryness of her tone. The cleanness of the castle had not occurred to him much. He should have known it would matter to a woman like Calliope. "I suppose you are right." He tightened his arm around her, hugging her more tightly and leaning down to brush his lips to the top of her head. "You were not brought here to act as a servant, little one. However, this is your home now as much as it is mine and Reinn's. You should feel comfortable to make it as you like. Have Reinn help you tomorrow."

"Reinn shall be here with me tomorrow then?"

What was it about Reinn that caused her spine to straighten? Bronwen looked down at her again, and waited for her to look up, but she simply lay where she was, her cheek on his chest, fingers twirling in his chest hairs, her body now as tight as the string on a bow.

"Did he not stay with you today?" Surely he had not left her alone. Reinn knew how dangerous the risk was. Even within the walls of the castle, they could not be certain of her safety without their presence. Demons knew Bronwen was certainly no protection for her in the daylight. Perhaps in the early hours just before dawn or the hour before sunset, but even then only when he kept to heavy shadows.

"He was here for a while when I woke." She yawned and he knew sleep would take her before long.

"But he left," he prodded. And she had gone about the castle on her own. What if she had gone out? What if someone had seen her? What if she had found him? "Did he at least stay most of the day?"

"No. I met him downstairs. We," she swallowed and yawned again though this time it sounded suspiciously forced, "talked for a minute then I came upstairs to dress. When I returned, he was gone."

Bronwen looked to the ceiling, his mind reeling, temper boiling and power sizzling just below the surface. He tempered it, forced it back, both unwilling to let himself loose it with her and unknowing how sensitive she might be to feeling his powers.

"Sleep now, little one," he whispered and kissed the top of her head again. He settled back to indulge himself in a time of simply holding her as she drifted to sleep. Later, he let a trickle of power glide over her to aid her in sleep before soundlessly slipping out of bed.

Chapter Four

Reinn stumbled several steps back, his head snapping hard as the blow landed squarely and quite painfully on his jaw.

"You had sex with her." Power radiated on the air, crawling over Reinn's skin as he bent at the waist, braced his hands on his knees and tried to focus around the pain. He had barely managed a swallow and a ragged breath, barely thought he might be able to straighten when another blow, this time to his nose, had him landing flat on his ass.

Blood splattered and flew. The beast inside him leapt to its paws, ready to pounce. He felt the change beginning in his feet and hands, the bones elongating and nails extending, and he knew when his gaze landed on Bronwen, the vampire would see the gold-rimmed green of his wolf's eyes darker by several degrees then the usual electric green of the man's eyes.

"Come on wolf." Bronwen sneered, his fangs already in full view, his own eyes scarlet red with blood and rage. "We will go monster to monster if you wish. Shift, dammit!"

Reinn fought for control, battling the beast inside him so he could think clearly. The urge to shift, to attack, to maim was stronger than he had felt in so very long. Friend, lover, Bronwen...the words flittered through his thoughts a split second before he gave into the change.

"No." The word roared from his throat, harsh and animalistic exactly like the beast he barely managed to keep on a leash inside him.

Bronwen advanced, slow and tempered strides, threatening, waiting. His fist clenched and unclenched at his sides. Even with the power slicing the air around them, he too managed a level of control nearly impossible to hold when so very angry.

Rein watched as Bronwen's fangs retreated behind the sexy sneer of his upper lip and damned himself for being so aroused by the sight of the man so angered he was likely to tear his throat out with his teeth. Literally. The fangs disappeared but the fury remained, the driving force to all that kept Bronwen going at that moment.

"Then get off your ass and fight me like a man." Bronwen reached Reinn in a speed almost too fast for the man he now spoke of being. He bent and fisted a pale hand in Reinn's shirt.

Reinn felt himself hauled to his feet before his mind could send message to his limbs to stand. Bronwen held him, his feet an inch from the ground, the vampire's face so close Reinn felt the absence of breath between them. Vampires did not need to breathe, but they could and Bronwen often did. Simply to feel the illusion of humanity, he had once told Reinn.

Though he claimed to wish to fight like a man, he was not looking for that human illusion now. The air between them was as still as a breezeless summer day, the heat nearly tangible.

Bronwen's strength could pulverize Reinn with a flick of the wrist. Reinn knew that and, sadistic monster that he was, a part of him rode on the thrill of that knowledge. Even supremely pissed and fighting for control, Bronwen exuded a sexual aura so blatant Reinn could almost taste it. He *wanted* to taste it.

Bronwen stood before him wearing only a pair of untied breeches, fine ebony pubic hairs shadowing his pale flesh at the open leather fly. All Reinn could think in that moment was how badly he longed to trace those unyielding muscles of Bronwen's bare chest and abdomen with his tongue, to run his hands over every inch of his pale enticing flesh, to nip and bite and feed. But it was the pain in Bronwen's eyes, the look of deception and grief that had Reinn's own beast settling, the lustful urges stopping in mid-swirl in his loins.

"I will not fight you, Bronwen," he whispered. "Not as man or wolf."

Bronwen's fist tightened around Reinn's shirt and he gave him a quick, vicious shake that had his brain rattling, another droplet of blood flying from his nose, and his bare toes grazing the floor.

"You had sex with her," Bronwen repeated, disbelief warring with the temper in his tone. He did not yell this time, nor did he whisper, but no matter the timbre, Reinn was certain the underlining pain could hurt no more than it did right now.

"I did." What more could he say? There was no point in attempting to deny what transpired between him and Calliope that morning. Less than five minutes alone with her and he had pinned her to the wall, fucked her until they were both equally breathless and speechless. Bronwen had to know. Ashamed as Reinn felt about his actions, sick as the desire to repeat it all again made him, Bronwen deserved the truth. "She is for me, too."

A muscle in Bronwen's angular jaw jumped, fire burning hot in his eyes, but shock replaced the temper in his expression in a finger snap succumbing to anger once more. "Did you think to anger me? To hurt me?" Bronwen pushed at Reinn.

Reinn stumbled two steps back, but managed to keep his footing.

"Did you think to hurt her? To make her run? What *were* you thinking?" Bronwen spun from him, stalked to the opposite side of the chamber, stomped back and began to pace.

"She is for me, too," Reinn tried again and this time his words got through. Bronwen stopped and for a long moment Reinn stared at the vampire's side profile, broad shoulders rigid, spine straight, chest and stomach utterly still. No ragged breaths racked him, no tremble from the temper shook him, no muscle moved at all. Reinn knew even as amazement, love and longing swept through him that he stared at a true standing corpse.

Bronwen finally moved, his head angling even as it turned to Reinn, ebony hair falling behind his cheek like a silken backdrop. The eyes were just as dark, the bloodlust gone now as the confusion and truth took root in his mind. "You feel for her, too?"

Reinn wiped at his nose with the back of his hand, flicked a glance at the blood, and ignored the growl of hunger low in his belly. "I do. I knew at the celebration when I stood with you and gazed upon her from the shadows. She is meant for me, too."

"You are certain of this?" Bronwen turned full to face Reinn now, his tone even, his body stiff but no longer poised to fight.

"It is a bone deep longing." Reinn turned his focus inside himself, remembering how he had felt the night outside the goddess queen's palace, the sheer unavoidable need that controlled him that morning when Calliope ended the stairs. "You sense it in your head, your heart, and your loins. There is no mistaking it, no ignoring it, no pretending you do not feel it." He knew the last for absolute certain for he tried all day to pretend he felt only contempt for the woman now living inside the walls of their castle. Just as he had pretended for more years than he cared to confess he felt only friendship for Bronwen. In truth, what he felt for the vampire was so mirroring that which rocked his senses at the sight of Calliope that he had been struck dumb by them both.

Bronwen shoved a hand through his hair. "I do not understand how this can be. I am not wrong in what I know, what I have always known."

"Nor am I in what I know now," Reinn countered with a sigh. "She is meant for us both and we are meant for her."

"How could the guardians be so cruel?" Bronwen sighed and let his hand fall to his side with a light slap of irritation.

"Why not?" Reinn shrugged and touched his jaw where Bronwen's first blow had connected. It hurt like a bitch in heat! "Fate was pissy enough to mate her with one of us. Why not both? I would have never had sex with her to hurt you, Bronwen."

Bronwen's gaze locked with his, the vampire's expression softening to one of apology and regret. "I know. I was angry. You should have punched me."

"Perhaps, but..." Reinn shrugged again as Bronwen walked to him. Reinn's heartbeat tripped with each step.

"Your jaw is already beginning to bruise." Bronwen grazed the back of his finger along Reinn's jaw and Reinn closed his eyes, loving the touch. "And you are bleeding still."

Reinn swiped at his nose again. It was already beginning to heal. Still, he winced at the low sting of lingering pain. "You pack a hell of a punch. I am lucky you did not break my neck with that one."

"As am I, my friend." Bronwen reached for Reinn's hand, stared at the blood streaking the flesh for a long, hunger arousing moment, and then brought the hand to his mouth, and licked.

He could not resist. He barely had a thought that he should. Reinn leaned in, licked at the blood too, so closely that his tongue glided alongside Bronwen's. The vampire did not jerk back in anger or surprise as Reinn might have expected. Instead, heart hammering at an almost painful pace, he watched as Bronwen pulled away slowly and straightened. It took a long time for his gaze to reach Reinn's eyes. The gradual climb it made had Reinn's cock so hard it pulsed between his legs, his mouth watering in hope, his tongue remembering that one quick feel of Bronwen's. The vampire still held his hand and he dared to lace their fingers together as he gathered a strength he always wished to have, *knew* he would need to accomplish this.

"You were jealous of her, because I had her, because I fucked her." Reinn could not take his own eyes off Bronwen's, needing to watch the emotions, the reactions. At the moment, the vampire kept them carefully blank.

"I had no right." Bronwen let a quick flash of guilt and regret move through his face. "She is obviously meant for us both."

"As you are." Blankness again. Reinn waited for another quick flash of something. When he saw none, he plunged on. "I was jealous of her, too. Because she had you." He dared to bring his free hand to Bronwen's cheek. "Because she fucked you."

It happened so fast Reinn did not even catch a flash of intention. Bronwen whirled Reinn around, slamming his back against the hard wall of Bronwen's body, one hand at Reinn's waist holding him close. All breath left Reinn's lungs. Bronwen may not need oxygen but he did and suddenly there did not seem to be enough in the chamber.

"Is it the same, old friend?" Bronwen's words whispered in Reinn's ear, low and with a seductive lilt Reinn was certain he had never heard from the vampire, at least not directed at him. "Do you feel it here?" At the question, Bronwen's free hand came up, the fingers grazing over Reinn's temple, his forehead, diving into his hair.

Reinn moaned, both wolf and man angling his head into the touch. His arms were at his sides, shock and wonder stiffening his muscles, rendering his arms immovable. Bronwen let the strands of Reinn's hair slide through his fingers, toying lightly with the curls.

"Do you feel it here?"

The hand cruised down Reinn's front in an agonizing slowness that had every fiber of his being solidifying. Reinn stood statue still against the vampire, unable to move, barely able to breathe as the hand stopped at Reinn's flat stomach.

"How about here?" On the move again, Bronwen slid his hand lower to cover Reinn's stiff cock.

Pleasure, excitement, torment, tore through Reinn in a wild disbelieving rush. How long had he dreamed of having Bronwen's hands on him this way? *Too long. Oh Gods, Far too long.*

"Yes." The word sounded strangled even to his own ears as he tilted his head and met Bronwen's exploring gaze. "I feel for you all of those places and more. It is the same and yet it is not. I—I am not sure I can explain."

"You do not have to." Bronwen bent his head, his lips so close to touching Reinn's. *So close.* The hand on Reinn's cock squeezed ever so slightly, a pulsing pressure of stupendous intensity. "I already know. I feel it, too."

Surprise had Reinn's eyes growing wide. He knew? He felt it, too? All the years of secretly hoping, wishing... "Why?"

"It had to be the three of us." Bronwen brushed his nose lightly to Reinn's, careful not to harm, only to tease.

Reinn felt the visceral effects of it sizzle through him like a lightning bolt of evil desire straight to his groin where Bronwen's hand lightly explored Reinn's bulging cock. "Ah, yes."

Bronwen's lips twitched. "I never knew for certain why I waited, why I led you to believe I did not know you care for me until I realized tonight we are meant to be three." He nipped Reinn's bottom lip and then licked the traces of blood Reinn knew were still smearing his face.

Reinn closed his eyes, unable to take it all in. This was Bronwen, the man he had wanted for centuries, the man he pined for by day and hide the truth from in the dark. "I love you." The words were out of his mouth before he could stop them, before he realized there was no need to stop them anymore, no need to hide.

"I know." Bronwen covered Reinn's mouth with his in a kiss so light and so quick Reinn wondered if he had been sucked back into his fantasies. *Please no.* "As I do you."

Reinn stared at him, unable to believe, afraid to hope he heard him right. When Bronwen let the smile unfold on his lips, let all the emotions he spoke of swim into the blackest depths of his eyes, Reinn knew it was okay to believe, okay to hope. "I want you."

Bronwen's palm ground the outside of Reinn's breeches, his cock beneath. "I know." He kissed him, this time coaxing Reinn's lips to part, his tongue diving inside for a slowly delicious kiss that had Rein trembling. "As I do you." His hand on Reinn's waist dipped to joining the other, to fumble with the ties of Reinn's breeches. All the while, they stared transfixed at each other, both lost in the moment, the anticipation, the love that was no longer secret between them.

"Tell me, wolf," Bronwen continued as his hand slipped inside Reinn's now unfastened breeches. The sound that rumbled from Reinn's throat as Bronwen closed his fingers around Reinn's shaft were ones he had never heard himself make before. Bronwen tugged Reinn's cock free then slowly and methodically started to stroke it from base to head. Reinn's vision blurred as arousal sliced through his nut sack, tightening his balls and seizing control of his hips. He thrust into Bronwen's hand, going mindless with the feel of the vampire jerking him off so skillfully. "Do you wish to be taken, lover, or to take?"

Reinn thought the choices to be one in the same, but he knew what Bronwen meant. He reached a hand back, shoving between their bodies and instantly found Bronwen's cock. He did not stop to toy and tease as Bronwen had done, but merely plunged a hand inside the other man's open breeches and enveloped the severe cool dick he found. Bronwen's sharp intake of breath pleased Reinn more than any words at that moment. For his touch to have such an effect on a vampire…

"I will be taken," Reinn decided, knowing Bronwen would give as much as he took. It was not the answer Bronwen expected and Reinn could not tell if Bronwen were pleased by that or wished it the other way. Before he could ask, Bronwen was kissing him again, his hands moving to the waist of Reinn's breeches, tugging them down his hips.

Reinn reached both hands behind him, fisted the leather of Bronwen's breeches and worked them down in the same way. At last, *Gods help him*, Bronwen's naked body pressed to his. The combination of hot and cold sent an excited fear skittering through his system. Bronwen's tongue caressed his mouth, gliding over his tongue then retreating to lick the outer rims of his lips. His hands moved, pulling Reinn's shirt up and breaking his laboring kisses only long enough to tug the shirt over Reinn's head. Then his hands were back on Reinn's body, starting at his shoulders and gliding their way down so infinitesimally slowly it had Reinn panting and writhing, his hand groping behind him in search of Bronwen's cock.

"Patience, my wolf." There was a hint of laughter in Bronwen's tone. He took a step back, carefully keeping his dick out of Reinn's reach.

"Bron-*wen*." Reinn growled the name but the last syllable stuck in his throat as Bronwen's fingers once again curled around his throbbing shaft.

"Is this not why you wished to be taken?" Bronwen nuzzled the side of Reinn's neck, his tongue licking the pulse point he found there.

Lust pooled in Reinn's gut, needs roared and his wolf reared, ready to pounce or to submit, he was not quite sure which.

"You wished our first time to be slow, did you not? You wished it to last."

He had. He did. It was one of several reasons for his decision. "I could change my mind." Reinn brought his arm up, curled it behind Bronwen's neck, needing both the contact and something to hold onto. Damn if his knees were not so weak he could hardly stand!

Bronwen's lips curved in a wicked and incredibly sexy grin as his hand fisted Reinn's cock just enough to have his eyes rolling back in his head. "It is too late for that, lover. For this one time if never again it is you who will submit to me." His free hand roamed Reinn's body, skimming over muscles, tracing ridges and lines, while the hand on Reinn's cock stroked and caressed.

"You are killing me, Bronwen." Reinn growled, his fingers digging into the flesh at Bronwen's nape. He managed to find purchase on Bronwen's hip with his other hand, but each time he attempted to feel more, Bronwen drew his lower body out of reach.

"Not yet."

There was a hint of fang in the smile Bronwen gave him this time and a ripple of eager alarm raced down his spine. Then Bronwen's roaming hand reached between their bodies, palmed Reinn's ass and a long, slender finger slid between his ass cheeks. Reinn stilled, muscles tensing, breath catching, heart beating wildly against his ribcage.

Bronwen nuzzled his neck as the pad of his finger grazed the outer rim of Reinn's anus. "Is there a problem, lover?"

"No." He was in sheer ecstasy. The feel of Bronwen exploring his anus filled him with such anticipation and wondrous sensations he was afraid to move. Bronwen eased the finger inside, working it in slow circles deeper and deeper, spreading Reinn's ass even as his other hand continued to stroke Reinn's cock.

Bronwen let out a low moan of utter appreciation. "You feel so good, lover. So tight and slick. Your muscles squeeze at my finger and my cock yearns for the same treatment."

"That is what I want." All that he wanted in that moment. To feel Bronwen take him, to feel Bronwen's thick and long cock shoving its way through the resistant muscles in his anus.

"Yes, I know." Bronwen pulled his finger free but, before Reinn could expel the sound of protest rising in his throat. Bronwen was working two fingers into his stretching hole. The pain, the pleasure, mixed in a concoction that drove Reinn closer to insanity than he had ever been. "You have always been the one for more immediate gratification, my wolf, while I prefer the thrill of anticipation. That is, as you have already agreed, why we are at this point now."

"I made a mistake," Reinn ground through gritted teeth. Pleasure spiked to an all new high as Bronwen's fingers buried deep inside his tight anus. He felt the fingers turn and wriggle, spread and caress, and his cock flexed as spasms built in his balls. "Do not make me come this way, Bronwen. I wish to feel you inside me when I come."

Bronwen released Reinn's cock but his fingers remained lodged deeply in Reinn's ass. "Yes, that is what I want as well. However, I am not through enjoying this moment, my wolf." He leaned down, licking a fiery chilled path along Reinn's shoulder, nipping his collarbone, dancing his tongue up the side of Reinn's neck.

"You will need to feed again before sunrise," Reinn managed around the rapidly increasing pumping of his pulse. Bronwen could smell it. Reinn knew he could for the beast inside himself smelled it too. Wolf and vampire, both hungered for blood each for their own reason, each for reasons that were identical. "Feed on me while you fuck me, Bronwen. Bring us both to bliss with your powers, your cock, your fangs."

"Your body," Bronwen added and pulled his fingers from Reinn's ass with a quiet pop. The men shared a smile as Bronwen's hands moved to Reinn's waist.

Reinn braced, his gaze welded to Bronwen's as the vampire folded his cool body around Reinn's and bent them both slightly forward. With a firm grip on Reinn's hips, Bronwen eased his cock inside, first between the tight ass cheeks and then straight into Reinn's anus without manipulation or guidance.

His breath left him on a hiss of pleasured pain as Bronwen's thick cock stretched his ass more than his fingers before. The slow speed in which Bronwen entered him heightened his every sense, sending pinpricks of sensations he could not define shooting through him to fall back like a rain of sharp arrows. Bronwen's cock rubbed at the sensitive walls of Reinn's anus, his fingers digging into flesh and bone on his hips as Bronwen took his ass inch by glorious inch.

"Ah, Gods."

Behind him, he heard Bronwen's echoing sigh, felt the vampire's rigid control as he no doubt fought the urge to plunge and pound, rather than coax and finesse. Still, Bronwen continued to fill him deeper and deeper until he was almost certain he couldn't take anymore. He was about to say so, about to tell Bronwen to stop, the pleasure was simply too much to form words, when he realized he didn't have to. Bronwen's lips cruised over the back of his shoulder, Bronwen's cock impossibly deep inside his ass.

"You feel..." Bronwen began but trailed off, pulled his hips back, and eased several rock hard inches out before gradually pushing in again. "So amazing. Your ass, the muscles as they close and clamp around my cock."

Reinn fought the urge to let go. In that moment, with Bronwen's erotic words, his lips against his flesh, his body inside his, Reinn nearly lost himself to the ejaculation that tightened his balls, thudded in his dick. "Now, Bronwen. Please."

"Please what, lover?"

He would make him beg for it? Reinn might have been astonished, angered even if the needs inside him hadn't built to near explosion. For any other man, any other person, he would not have done it. But this was Bronwen, the man he had wanted for far too long to deny himself now. "Fuck me, bleed me, make me come."

Reinn felt the slight brush of sharp point to tender flesh just before Bronwen's fangs pierced the pulsing vein in the side of his neck. The combination was exquisite, Bronwen drinking from his neck, Bronwen fucking his ass, Bronwen reaching with his free hand to find his cock once more. He stroked it in long and pressured squeezes until Reinn saw nothing but white-hot lights of bursting rapture as his hips met Bronwen's thrust for generous thrust. All of it so painstakingly tender in its way. All of it so marvelously pushing the edge of everything wicked and sweet. Every awareness magnified by Bronwen's power as it glided over their bodies, driving Reinn's senses to a dynamic earth-shattering fulfillment.

They erupted together, Bronwen shooting his seed into Reinn's ass, Reinn coming in a burst of sticky sweet goo into Bronwen's hand. Breath ragged, muscles liquidized, Reinn let Bronwen take much of his weight. Slowly, Bronwen let his cock slip from Reinn's now tender hole and only then did Reinn find the strength to open his eyes. He found Bronwen gazed down at him, his mouth covered in Reinn's blood, his expression a cross between wicked satisfaction and gentle love. His hand released Reinn's dick and he brought it up, the glimmer of the candlelight in the chamber glistening like sparkles of diamonds off the come that covered his flesh.

Gaze locked with Reinn's, Bronwen licked his palm, made an, "Mmm," sound, and then offered it to Reinn. "Will you taste yourself, lover?"

Reinn closed his hand over Bronwen's offered one and turned in the vampire's arms. "I would rather taste it on you." Snaking his free hand behind Bronwen's neck, he pulled him down for a kiss, tasting both his own blood and his semen in the vampire's mouth.

* * * *

"You surprised me tonight, lover." Bronwen sat with his back against the headboard of Reinn's bed, his arms draped over Reinn's broad shoulders, his hands idly caressing the smooth hairless skin of Reinn's chest.

Reinn sat between his legs, his back leaning against Bronwen's front, his hands offering the same caressing comfort to Bronwen's outstretched legs on either side of Reinn's body. At Bronwen's words, Reinn tipped his head back, a mischievous grin spreading his lips.

Bronwen chuckled and shook his head. "When did you become such a submissive lover, my wolf?" Reinn's grin turned serious, sultry, arousing. Bronwen gazed down at him, picturing just for a moment those lips closing around his cock, that mouth sucking him deep, demanding he come.

"When you put your hands on me."

He said it so seriously Bronwen felt the words wrap around his lifeless heart. Lifeless? No. His heart may not beat but it was far from unresponsive. He had found that out tonight first with Calliope and now with Reinn. Both of his hearts held him close tonight, both of his hearts allowed him to claim them as his.

"You were always the more aggressive one," Bronwen muttered and grazed the backs of his fingers down Reinn's warm cheek.

"I still am. Do not despair, white knight. I shall prove my dominance next time."

"White knight?" Bronwen arched a brow, the corner of his lips twitching.

Reinn lifted Bronwen's arm and held it up for inspection. "They do not come much whiter than you." He brushed his lips to Bronwen's flesh, his tongue snaking out for a lick that had Bronwen leaning his head back and pushing an airless breath from his pursed lips. Reinn laughed. "Ah, but I do love the effect I have on you tonight."

"Have always had on me," Bronwen corrected, lifting his head. "I am sorry now that I waited so long to let you know."

"I know now." Reinn shrugged. "That is what matters. She will have to know, too." His eyes narrowed. "Or do you intend to keep this a secret from her?"

"Even if that were my intention, how could I when we are both meant for her?"

Reinn nodded and settled back against Bronwen's chest. "I was pretty rough with her this morning." He chuckled but the sound held little humor. "No submissive wolf there. Did I hurt her? Did she tell you if I hurt her?"

"She made little mention of you." Bronwen slid fingers through Reinn's hair, loving the way the silken curls twisted around his fingers as though trying to keep them there.

"Ouch!" Reinn winced. "I suppose I did not make a lasting impression."

Bronwen laughed. "Quite the opposite I am sure, lover. I believe she was taken aback by the appearance of two of us."

"You mean the whole quivering to her toes thing when she met me this morning and then you walked into her chamber tonight?"

"She believed I was you at first. She was sitting before the mirror when I entered, combing her hair in such a way that had my dick attempting to tie itself in knots." The mere memory of watching the gentleness in which she stroked her hair had his dick tingling in response even now.

"She seems to have that effect. More, she appears not to even realize the true effect she possesses."

"Of that, I can agree. You left her alone today." He had not meant to sound so accusing but the words, the tone, spilled before he could alter them.

Reinn tensed slightly in his arms, and then visibly relaxed before he spoke. "I watched over her. She was never out of my sight."

"Watching from the shadows, were you?"

"I learned from the master." Reinn shot him a quick grin. "She cleaned!"

The genuine astonishment in Reinn's voice had Bronwen smiling back. "So she said. She also mentioned you do not keep a very tidy home."

"Oh she did, did she?" Reinn narrowed his eyes, his lip protruding in a bit of a feigned pout.

"You cannot deny she is right."

"I suppose not. I could not leave her. Not just because of the danger we believe awaits her, but because I simply could not stand to be away. Yet, I could not stay with her either. After the way I nailed her in the foyer and—"

"The foyer? You could not have the decency to take the woman to a bed?"

"I could not think what I was doing let alone what I should have been doing, Bronwen. She, Gods, she does something to you and it is…"

"Exquisite, arousing, magnificent," Bronwen supplied.

"Pick one. They all work. And I was pissed. I did not want to want her. I wanted you and she had you."

"You were that jealous?" Bronwen could not hide the hint of pleasure mixed with amusement he heard in his own voice at that.

"Go ahead. Lap it up, vampire," Reinn said dryly. "The fact is it tore me apart, knowing I had taken what belonged to you, knowing she had what I wanted most."

"We, the three of us, belong to each other." Bronwen folded his arms around Reinn's neck, rested his brow on the top of Reinn's head, and hugged the other man close. "That was you tonight, the wolf's howl when I was with Calliope. That was you."

Reinn nodded. "I couldn't stand knowing what was happening in that chamber. I couldn't stand that she was having you and not me."

"But you were not jealous of me having her?" As he waited for Reinn's answer, he turned the question around on himself. Was he jealous of Calliope having Reinn? Yes, he decided. The answer was yes. Perhaps not as intensely, he reluctantly admitted, for it was Calliope who held seventy-five percent of his heart in that way. But the other twenty-five percent belonged only to Reinn. Would he be willing to share Reinn with any other than Calliope? Absolutely not! The mere idea had him turning his lips into Reinn's head, brushing them over the crown in assurance the man remained his.

"I was, but not in the same way. I—"

"It is okay, lover. You do not have to explain."

"Good because I am not sure I can."

"You nailed her in the foyer." Bronwen shook his head, unable to get passed the wolf's lack of control. It was stimulating, to say the least. "You must show me how that is done some time."

Reinn shifted to lie on his side and reached a hand between Bronwen's legs to cover his cock. "I could show you now."

Bronwen bit back an oath. The warmth of Reinn's hand enclosing his cock, the thumb rubbing lightly over the most sensitive strip of flesh between his shaft and balls drove him mindless. "The sun will be upon us soon, lover," he managed through gritted teeth.

Reinn's face fell, his lips grazing over Bronwen's abdomen and stomach. Bronwen's muscles tensed, almost painful spasms of need ricocheting through his cock.

"I know," Reinn whispered. "I find myself wishing for the first time ever that the dark would not end."

Bronwen often found himself wishing the same. More, he wished he could walk in the light. It had been so long since he had seen true light, since he felt the heat of the sun upon his flesh, the comfort of the day and all its ability to wash away the terrors of night.

Needing that comfort tonight more than he had in so very long, he bent his head to Reinn and brushed a light kiss to the other man's lips. "Will you stay with me in my chamber until sunrise?"

"Why not stay here instead? You will be safe in my chamber through the day. I will make sure of it."

Bronwen nodded. He knew Reinn would never allow anything to happen to his lifeless body in the light. "Then hold me, lover, and I shall hold you until the ability to do so leaves me for a time."

They slid down to lay flat on the bed, arms holding tight, legs entwined until Reinn drifted to sleep and the sun rose to steal Bronwen's existence.

Chapter Five

Hands glided over Calliope's flesh, urgent and demanding. Her body arched into their touch, quiet moans escaping her throat as they grazed over her breasts, her pussy, her ass. Bronwen leaned in, his mouth closing over her breast, his teeth clamping down on her nipple. Between her legs, Reinn positioned his cock to enter her eager pussy even as Bronwen's hand pushed between her bottom and the mattress, a finger shoving inside her butt cheeks to graze over her anus.

She writhed, twisted, and feigned resistance against the pleasure that rocked her so viciously she thought she might be close to death. Her head came up; the desire to watch what they did to her body overriding her needs to lay flat.

What she saw instead had a scream tearing from her throat.

Animals. No, not just any animals but wolves surrounded her, monstrous snarling wolves with jagged razor sharp teeth and evil yellowish-golden eyes. They moved in a slow circle around her as if in a predatory dance of ritual and sacrifice. Somehow she knew she was that sacrifice!

The man at her breast moved, sitting back to sneer down at her. Not Bronwen, her frantic mind realized. Fangs protruded from the mouth of a beast, not man, not animal, the features indistinguishable. Her gaze flicked to the man between her legs. Not Reinn either but another beast, this one half man and half animal. Half wolf!

"You should not have come here." The half wolf rasped, the derision in his tone grating her flesh like a harsh rock. "The dark is no place for a demigoddess."

"You are ours now," the fanged thing declared. His hands closed over her breasts, nails long and filthy digging into the sensitive flesh. "And we will keep you ours forever."

They grinned, devious and horrid smiles that dripped with venom and malice as the leaned down, one between her legs, the other toward her throat, their mouths opened, teeth bared to bite.

Calliope awoke on a strangled scream. She bolted upright in the bed, heart hammering wildly against her breast bone, her breath coming in rapid and loud burst. A dream, she realized as she frantically scanned the chamber. Only when she discovered she was indeed alone in the faintly growing sunlight did she begin to calm.

"Just a dream," she whispered aloud and forced herself to take deep calming breaths to slow her pounding heart. "A nightmare."

When the relief washed through her, she fell back on the bed, one hand coming up to cover her heart. She could still feel it drumming insistently beneath her palm. It was definitely not her preferred way to wake in the morning.

Too revolted by the memory of the beasts and what they did to her to dwell on the whys of exactly what caused her to dream such a horrid thing, she pushed the nightmare aside and slid from the bed. Her legs were wobbly, the lingering adrenaline rush of fear propelling her more than her own muscle's abilities to move at that moment.

She was reaching for the robe draped over the knob of one of the foot bedposts when the knock sounded at the door. Before she could think to call to her visitor or cover herself or hide, the door swung open and Reinn ambled inside. He carried a tray laden with dishes. He had pulled his curls back, tying them at his nape. His chest was bare, leaving hairless pecs and abdomen gleaming in an exhibit of pure male beauty. He wore a pair of brown breeches made from some sort of animal hide though decidedly not leather and his feet were bare.

"I thought I would bring breakfast to you this morning." He headed straight for a table beneath the window and set down the tray.

"Call it a peace offering, an apology for leaving you alone on your first day in your new home."

Calliope blinked. In three seconds he had said more words to her than he said all of yesterday. Perhaps he had simply needed some time to adjust to having a woman in the house. Or maybe he knew she had been with Bronwen last night.

"Did you sleep well?" He turned, a small knowing grin tilting his lips but when his gaze landed on her the grin faded. "What is wrong? You are pale. Are you sick? Has something happened?" He was in front of her in an instant, his hands gripping her shoulders firmly.

"I am fine," she hastened to assure him. "A bad dream. That is all."

"A bad dream?" He narrowed his eyes, angling his head. "Tell me."

"I do not wish to tell you." She stepped back. He could have stopped her but instead let her go. "It was too," she shook her head, "ugly. I do not wish to remember it enough to put it to voice."

He watched her for several heartbeats as if weighing the benefits of pushing the issue. Finally, he nodded and sighed. "Very well, as long as you are okay now."

"I am fine," she repeated and smiled. It was the truth, she realized. She was fine now that he was with her. She felt so secure in his presence. She could not say exactly why. She had, after all, only spent a precious few minutes with him yesterday morning. It was simply something about him, a protectiveness that radiated from his gorgeous body that left her feeling as though nothing would ever happen to her as long as he were around.

"Will you join me for breakfast?" He shot a glance at the table where the breakfast tray sat, then looked back at her in question.

As if in answer, her stomach gave a loud and decided growl. He grinned and the sultry tilt of his lips grazed over every erogenous point in her body. Any lingering horrors that remained in her mind from the nightmare vanished in a puff of sexual smoke as she filled her vision with the sight of his smooth, bare chest, his rippling abdomen, the faint hint of pubic hair just visible at the band of the low-riding breeches.

"I suppose I am hungrier than I realized." *For both the food and you.* By the guardians, she was becoming a sex addict!

He led her to the table and pulled out her chair. She studied him as she sat, though she was careful to keep her mind pure, her gaze on his face rather than his truly appetizing body. "You seem different today," she commented as he took the liberty of serving her, loading her plate with fruits, cheeses, bread and creams.

"Why? Because I did not jump your bones as soon as I entered the room?" Though his tone held a hint of sarcasm, the grin he shot her was playful and mischievous.

"Well, there is that." She picked up her goblet of juice and watched him over the rim as she sipped. "Jump my bones, what an interesting phrase. My sister, Karan, would love it."

"I was rude to you yesterday. I apologize. I felt," he hesitated, his gaze dropping to his plate, "things when I looked at you that I had not expected to feel."

"Would it be wrong of me to say I liked the way you handled those feelings, at least at first."

He chuckled, a sound of both surprise and utter amusement. "There have been rumors of you and your sisters, stories of your beauty, your personalities." He sipped from his goblet and put it back on the table. "I must say, Calliope, while those stories did nothing to depict the full extent of your beauty, they were completely wrong about your personality."

"The innocent, unsuspecting, timid romantic." Calliope scowled and speared a piece of fruit with her fork. "I know what is said about me and most is right."

"I don't think so." Reinn shook his head. "From what I have seen, you are far from timid."

Only with you. Though the thought came quick, she caught the words on the tip of her tongue. And Bronwen. She had not been timid with Bronwen last night. And where had he gone? What was it with the two men in her life bringing her to an orgasm so ferocious and shattering then leaving her alone when it ended? She fell asleep in Bronwen's arms only to awaken sometime later alone in her bed.

"Where is Bronwen?" Something flashed through Reinn's eyes she could not identify. Jealously? Anger? Irritation? Neither seemed exactly right. Did he know she had sex with Bronwen last night? That Bronwen, to use Reinn's lovely term, jumped her bones in this very room? Did he know he was not the only man of the castle who felt the quivering knowledge of destined mating for her? Did he truly feel that quiver as she felt for him or had he simply used the premise as a way to have sex with her the previous morning?

She mentally scratched out the last question, knowing the answer with barely a thought. Of course he felt it too. He would not be here this morning if yesterday had simply been a ploy.

"He is away for the day. He had business to tend to." He hesitated briefly on the word business but plowed on. "I am certain he will come to you again tonight."

"Business," she repeated. "As you did yesterday?"

"Something like that. Today, however, I intend to spend the day with you. If you have no objections, of course."

Her belly flipped, sparks and tingles vying for paramount reaction in her veins. "I can think of none."

"I am told you cleaned the castle yesterday." Reinn settled back, his gaze studying her much as she did him when they sat.

She shrugged. "The chambers of the lower floor."

"You are to know that is not your job in the castle. It is not expected of you."

Calliope bit the inside of her cheek. "Perhaps not, but someone needs to. I am told," she turned his own words around on him, "that it is your job. I must say, you are not good at that job at all."

"My hands work better at other things." He scowled.

"Oh, I can agree with that."

* * * *

Reinn felt heat rise to his cheeks. No way was he blushing. Damn but she was nothing like he thought her to be. The innocent, unsuspecting, timid romantic sister, his ass. There was nothing innocent about her. Unsuspecting, perhaps. She knew not what lay in store for her in this castle, in the grounds beyond. Timid? At first, maybe, but she lost that rather quickly. As for the romantic aspect, he figured Bronwen would find the most enjoyment in that.

"I could refresh your memory if it fails this morning." His certainly hadn't. The feel of her soft, curvy body forming to his rigidly hard frame, her slick heated pussy clamped around his cock remained as fresh in his mind as it had been seconds after he fucked her. Even so, that did not mean he wasn't quite ready to do it again.

"It might." She angled her head and gazed at him under long blondish lashes. Teasing him, he knew and felt the effects squeeze at his balls. Oh no, there was nothing shy remaining about his woman.

She stabbed a piece of melon, licked it with the barest tip of her tongue before closing her lips around the chunk, tugging it off the fork with her teeth. All the while, her gaze lingered on his.

Spasms tightened his cock, his imagination putting his length in place of that bit of melon. "How about you come over here and do that?"

Saying nothing, she rose and walked around the table to him. He opened his legs. She stepped between them and put her hands on his shoulders. There were nerves in the touch, a slight tremble of her hands that the seductive expression on her face did not reveal. She licked her lips and his cock felt the slow, imagined glide from base to head.

"What is it you wish from me?" Her voice was as seductive as her face, a low and creamy caress that quivered only the slightest as she bent forward to brush those sultry lips to his.

He did not touch her. A part of him feared if he did he might unleash the shyness of which she spoke. Right now, she was in control, an alluring vixen with a devious gleam in her cornflower eyes and a wicked intent on her succulent lips. He started not to answer her question for the same fear, but he decided as she licked the outline of his lips, that since she had asked he would tell her exactly what he wished.

"Treat my cock as you did that melon. Suck me hard and fast and deep." He watched in amused fascination as his erotic words had her eyes darkening, and then glazing over.

Her hands cruised down the front of his shoulders, palms splaying over his pecs as her lips and tongue followed suit. She licked her way down his jaw, his neck, over his collarbone, all the while sinking to her knees between his legs.

By the time her hands reached his waist, her mouth had made it as far as his abdomen. He was gripping the side of the chair so hard it was a wonder the wood did not snap in his fingers. Her tongue delved into his bellybutton, teeth grazing and nipping the outer rim as her hands busied themselves with the ties of his breeches.

Her fingers closed around his shaft first, fisting the thick, throbbing rod as she pulled it free of his breeches. Her tongue continued on its downward path, lapping at the flesh of his stomach, the hairier flesh of his groin. By the time she stopped just short of those amazing lips reaching his cock, his breath was coming in labored intervals, his balls so stiff and stinging they felt as though a whip had been laid across them.

To his tormented dismay, she drew away, sat back on her heels, and gazed up at him. Her lips were moist from her sample of his body and tilted in a sexy as hell grin.

"Are you attempting to make me beg?"

She laughed, a short, amused sound that was both marginally embarrassed and a little thoughtful. "I am experimenting." Her gaze left his, a tinge of pink coloring her cheeks. "Is that a problem? Shall I stop?"

"I would be devastated if you did." Reinn managed to peel his fingers from the chair to reach for her. He cupped her cheek and drew her gaze back to his. Bolder by far, yes, but fragile. So very fragile. She had built strength to go this far. He did not want to see that strength shattered like glass.

"My body belongs to you at the moment. Do with it as you please, but know this, my lady, I too have experimenting I wish to do. When you are finished it will be my turn."

Arousal, white-hot and intense, broke through the uncertainty in her eyes. It was the embarrassment, the indecision he saw shatter like glass as her lips parted, as her face lowered, as she closed those lips around the head of his cock. She took no more of him than that, her tongue circling the tip, delving inside the slit to lap at the pre-cum leaking from the riot of glorious sparks and sizzles her lips sent through his shaft. Her lips flexed, squeezing down and then easing back, milking his head until his shaft screamed for the same treatment.

"Calliope, ah, Gods!" He sucked a breath through pursed lips as her teeth grazed the fold where head met with shaft. She bit just enough to draw a strangled cry from low in his throat. The pain laced pleasure had his hand diving into her hair, unable to not touch any longer.

She made an, "*Mmm,*" sound followed by a slurping noise as her tongue once again cleaned his head of the pre-cum and then sucked him down, head and shaft damned near to the base in one quick, teeth-jarring dive.

"Ah, shit!" Reinn fisted his hand in her hair even as he fought his body's need to control the motion of her head. He regretted that fight a half a second later when her head lifted, teeth and tongue grazing along the underside of his cock until it slipped entirely out of the warm paradise of her mouth.

"No!" Later he might be embarrassed by the sudden plea her action pulled from him but just now, with his balls aching as if stung by a dozen yellow jackets and his cock sizzling from the white-hot flames clawing his shaft, he cared not. He would plead, beg if that was what it took, to have her mouth on his cock again.

Her hair fell around her face like a golden curtain of silk, caressing his inner thighs as she dipped farther and sucked his balls into her mouth. She rolled them with her lips and tongue, hummed around them and the vibration skittered up his body and straight to his head, rattling his brain.

Her hand closed around his shaft as she fed on his balls, cradling his sac with her tongue and doing so many superb things with her mouth he was lost in the supreme sensations of it all. Her hand pumped his shaft, a pressured squeeze that had his release building in every part of his groin.

Do not make me come this way. He wanted to tell her even as he fought to hold back. He wanted to go in her mouth, to feel the sleek warmth around his cock as he shot his seed into her. She seemed to know he was close, seemed to want exactly as he because she suddenly jerked back, letting his balls fall from her lips and moved quickly, sinking his cock into her mouth once more.

She sucked him shallow at first, quick in and out slides, while her lips created a vise around his cock that had his eyes rolling in his head. Her speed increased slowly, measured thrusts that took his cock deeper inch by inch. He actually felt the muscles in her mouth, tongue and throat relax just before she swallowed his full length, her lips brushing against the base of his body.

It felt amazing, exquisite, the sheer pleasure of the pulsing sensations surrounding his cock, the pressure that flexed and milked until his balls tensed and the come burst from him on a ragged howl. His body jerked, his cock convulsed, his vision blurred. In that single moment, he lost complete control of every muscle, every thought, ever sense.

Calliope continued to suck him, drinking him down until he was spent and quivering with the exertion. As his shaft began to grow soft, she slowly eased back and gently let his cock fall from her devious lips.

Reinn opened eyes he had not realized he'd closed, waited while they focused, and then he blinked. She had gotten to her feet in front of him and gazed down at him now, an expression of indescribable hunger and sheer satisfaction on her amazing face. She licked her lips, a slow slide of her tongue tasting the overflow of her saliva, of his come. His cock ached at the sight, too spent to grow hard but too alive to not have some reaction.

"Should I allow you time to recover?" There was teasing in her voice and not of the seductive kind. Her lips twitched but it was her eyes that smiled.

In a lightning fast move that had those mesmerizing eyes widening and a shriek of surprise sounding from her lips, Reinn got out of the chair, caught her by the waist, and spun her around. He yanked her back against him, loving the way that shriek gave way to a catch of breath and a moan of pleasure.

"I suppose not."

"I recover quickly." He leaned in, nuzzled his face in the spill of hair at her neck, breathed in her incredible scent as his hands immediately began to work on removing her gown. He slid the straps of the midnight blue satin off her shoulders, pushing her hair aside with his nose so he could trail kisses over the flesh he exposed.

She moaned, her body swaying against him in a slow grinding dance as his mouth followed the material down her back, his tongue tracing the bumpy curves of her spine. She shivered and made the sexiest moaning sound.

The material fell in a pool around her feet. Reinn stopped his perusal of his tongue at the small of her back just above her exquisite heart-shaped ass. He splayed his hands over her warm cheeks, loving the smooth firm feel to his palms. A perfect fit, he thought and the idea of taking her there, of sinking his cock into her tight ass had him growing hard once more.

He resisted, trailing his hands up her back, her sides as he got to his feet. His arms moved around her waist and he lifted her, reaching to grab the dish of melon from the table before he carried her to the bed.

* * * *

Reinn carried her as if she weighed no more than a feather. The feel of his strong, muscular arms around her waist, of his hard warm body at her back was such an incredibly turn-on. Not that she needed any more of an aphrodisiac than she had already gotten. Sucking his cock, tasting his seed, made her pussy sopping wet and so very achy. She had very nearly come with him as his release slid down her throat.

He placed her on her stomach on the side of the bed, his hand stopping her when she attempted to crawl forward or roll over.

"Stay." The command was not harsh or gruff but firm enough she did not think to argue. "I want you just this way."

Her lower body from the waist down dangled over the side of the bed. The silk sheets felt cold to her beaded nipples and they hardened more in response. She turned her head to the side, lie on one cheek and put her hands on either side near her face. Though she could not see him, she felt his presence behind her, knew he looked upon her naked backside.

"Spread your legs for me." His hand pushed between her thighs and urged her legs to part.

The erotic command, the feeling of being exposed to his sight ignited the flames in her pussy. They licked at her core, freeing her feminine juices to run from between her already saturated folds.

"That's it," he said appreciatively. "So beautiful. You have an amazing pussy, Calliope. It is so wet just now. I can see your juices glistening on the sweet lips. Tell me, my lady, are those for me."

"Yes." The word was barely an audible whisper. The urge to close her legs had them quivering slightly but his body wedged between them prevented any such movement.

"Your flesh glows pink at my words. Do they embarrass you?"

They did. She felt the heat over every ounce of her body, embarrassment mixed with arousal. "Yes."

His palms glided over her ass and her backside jerked from the touch. He chuckled softly. "Such a lovely ass and a very enticing pale pink from your shyness too. I wonder how deliciously pink it would become under my hand. I wonder if such an erotic display would turn you on."

Calliope did not answer. Did he mean to spank her? Surely not!

"Another time, perhaps." He sounded thoughtful as his hands continued to glide over her ass. "However, I find myself unable to completely ignore the sweet curves."

Something wet, a combination of hot and cold, swiped down one of her butt cheeks followed instantly by the graze of something sharp. Calliope sucked in a breath, her body wiggling in reflex. His tongue and teeth. He had licked her, and then bit ever so slightly.

Reinn laughed. "Ah yes. You are a tasty one." Fingers spread her cheeks and a breeze drifted over the warmth of her crack. "Your pussy is almost dripping, you are so wet." He sounded delighted by that. Calliope did not know if she should be pleased or embarrassed.

She felt him move, felt one hand leave her bottom, then something as cold as ice lightly pressed to her clit and swiped from front to back between her saturated folds. Goose pimples covered her flesh and her breaths skittered out of her lungs. What was he doing to her? Gods, whatever it was felt amazing!

"Mmm, pussy flavored melon," he said around what was obviously a chunk of melon from their breakfast in his mouth. He repeated the movement with another chunk, this time pushing it just inside her aching opening as he slid the melon between her pussy lips. His body was warm and rigid against her back as he folded himself over her. "Would you like a taste?"

She opened her mouth but he shoved the bite of melon inside before she could utter a response. It, too, was a mixture of cold and hot, the melon cool and coated with the warm liquid of her body. It tasted gooey, thick, and a bit sweet. Nothing like his come had tasted and still not all together unpleasant. She would never admit that aloud.

"Your shyness is returning, my lady." He was leaning over her so she could see only his face and a few stray curls that had come free of their binding. He grinned, both playful and devious, one finger tracing the outline of her lips as she chewed the melon, then swallowed. "You like what I do to you, don't you? You like it, but you will not say it because it embarrasses you."

It did. She did. Was it not dirty and wrong to enjoy such reckless and wicked treatment? Bronwen had not taken her this way. He had been gentle, tender, sweet and caring and she had loved it. The memory of his touch, of his easy caresses stayed with her even now when her body ached with evil desires for another man. Another man who, like Bronwen, was her destined.

Calliope knew not how that could be, how both men could be her true heart. Just now, with so many sensations running ramped through her mind and body, no way could she contemplate the situation. She had loved being with Bronwen last night, reveled in the way he had treated her like a delicate object of his heart. Still, the fact remained, that she loved being with Reinn, too. A devious part of her thrilled on the command, the rough abandon in which he touched her, took her, claimed her.

"It is okay to enjoy such pleasures of the flesh, my lady." Reinn bent down and grazed his lips over her cheek. She smelled herself on his breath, the remnants of his own bite of melon. "Stay here," he whispered and pulled away.

He slithered down her body, slinking between her legs once more, spreading them far open with his hand on her inner thighs. She felt the warmth of his breath on her sex first, a split second before his tongue. He licked her from clit to anus in one swipe that had her hips coming off the bed. He gave a low growl, the sound so animalistic it rippled over her flesh in excited waves.

"Delicious! It seems I did not get enough breakfast, my lady. Allow me now to eat my fill."

As if she could have stopped him. As if she would have. He gave her no chance to respond, instead flipping her onto her back and drawing her legs to his shoulders. Before she could think, before she could even register the new position, his face disappeared between her legs. His fingers spread her saturated folds and his mouth covered her open sex.

Pleasure, incredible rioting rapturous shards of dagger sharp pleasure, speared through her much like the tongue that delved into her flaming channel. He fucked her with his tongue in vicious, unmeasured thrusts, the speed almost violent in its intensity. She gasped, writhed, and bucked against his face. His tongue retreated only long enough to move to her already swollen clit, to draw it between his teeth for a tender but pressured nip that had her crying out on a strangled scream. Then his tongue returned to its almost brutal attack on her opening.

The orgasm built, brutal and intense. It lingered just on the edge of release, a gigantic explosion awaiting just the right move, just the right touch for nuclear detonation.

"Please." The word was barely a whisper for she could speak no louder. All her focus, all her energy had centered between her legs, in her core where the orgasm hung in the balance. "Oh, Gods!"

Reinn yanked his tongue free, replacing it with two fingers diving deep inside her. Then he dipped further, his tongue tracing the ultra sensitive skin between her pussy and anus.

Calliope's breath quickened, her hips pumping against the fingers inside her, wanting them deeper, harder, looking for that exact touch to bring her the relief she so desperately sought. "Reinn, please! I am almost there but…"

He lifted her buttocks with his free hand, somehow simultaneously spreading her cheeks. When his tongue raked over her anus and then plunged inside, she came unglued. She cried out, writhing harder now, more out of control than ever before. She had never been touched there and the feel of his tongue penetrating such a secretively sensitive area of her body heated her to the point of boiling. She could not think, could not even find it within herself to be embarrassed by the act.

He feasted, on her pussy, her ass. There was no other word for it. And when at last he managed to pay attention to all three—the pad of his thumb grinding lightly over her clit, two slender and incredibly long fingers pumping in and out of her channel, a wide and exquisitely wet tongue probing her anus—she tumbled past the point of insanity. The combination was exactly the touch needed and so much more. She exploded so violently, her body racked with uncontrollable spasms so vicious she feared she lost conscience for a moment. Between her legs, somewhere buried below, she heard Reinn's low and satisfied growl before she tuned it all out and lost herself in the convulsing aftermath of her release.

Chapter Six

"Where are you going, little one?"

Calliope's heart gave one hard slam against her breastbone, the question jolting her as she turned from the front door and watched Bronwen's descent on the massive staircase. Lust pooled, pumping her juices, quivering her insides. His ebony hair was pulled back at his nape much as Reinn often wore his. The look accented the oval shape of his face, the high cheekbones, black eyes, and siren lips. He wore black—black breeches, black shirt, and black boots. It was such a contrast to his pale skin and so very sexy her heart began to pound for an entirely different reason.

"I thought I would walk outside." She hated the uncertainty that rose with her voice, knew there was no reason for the old shyness to return. Not with Bronwen. Not with either of her men. It was the expression on his handsome face that did it, the disapproving, suspicious, almost angry glint in his eyes that brought all her inhibitions back. She drew her bottom lip between her teeth and hoped he could not see it tremble. "Perhaps you would join me."

"I had other plans for tonight." He took her hand from the doorknob and brought it to his lips to brush it lightly with a kiss. "Perhaps you could postpone your outing and be with me instead."

"Of course." Though she felt disappointment, she fought not to let it show. Naturally she would want to be with him no matter the location whenever he chose. He was gone so often, after all. His business, whatever the sort, kept him from the castle well into the early evening every day. It was only now, hours after night fall that she got to spend time in his company.

Still, she longed for the outdoors. Over a week had passed since her arrival to the castle and she had yet to leave its walls. It had not bothered her at first. Reinn had taken to keeping her busy with cleaning and redecorating in the day, when he was not cornering her in some not so secluded area of the castle for hot, sweaty sex, and Bronwen entertained her with thoughtful conversation, romance and tender sex at night. Today, however, the urge for fresh air, for a walk among the grounds beneath the sun or even a starry sky weighed in her desires.

Bronwen led her to the great room where he had spread a throw over the floor before the roaring fireplace. Candle flames danced in time with that of the fire from tall crystal holders strategically placed on the floor by the throw. Goblets sat by one of those candles, presumably filled with his favorite red grape wine he often drank.

"I thought we could share conversation and drink by the warmth of the fire." Holding her hand, he yanked her arm gently, spinning her until she collided with the solid wall of his body. "Though I hope you will indulge me in a moment of closeness before we sit."

His arms enveloped her, his scent overwhelming, and she could not think to resist. He smelled of musk, of night, of fresh air, and she knew he had been outside just before coming to her. She wanted to ask where he had gone, where he spent his days, but not wanting to spoil the mood, she refrained.

Instead, she settled into him and let herself feel his presence as he began to sway, as her mind began to wander. She could not refrain forever. Sooner or later they would need to discuss things. In all the conversation they shared they had not once talked of many important things nagging at her of late. Things such as him and Reinn, of her and Reinn. Did Bronwen know of her daytime affair with Reinn? Bronwen was the master of the castle. How did he acquire it? Where was his family? What was his place as master? What was hers?

"You are thinking hard this night, little one." Bronwen's lips grazed the top of her head where her cheek rested on his chest. "Are you troubled?"

She was. Not so much troubled but curious, she supposed. But how to bring up all that boggled her? He had said he wished to share conversation by the fire. Perhaps he planned to answer many of her questions tonight. She would wait, she decided. Bide her time and see what happened.

"I was enjoying the dance," she told him by way of answer. "We did not get the opportunity to dance at the joining celebration."

His arms tightened around her waist, hugging her closer, and one hand began to caress up and down her back. "It was meant to be a special night for you. The most anticipated of your life."

"And of yours. Certainly the most exciting, anyway."

"I ruined that." He pulled back, reached to hook a finger beneath her chin, and lifted her face to look at him. "I am sorry for that."

The sincerity in his eyes diminished any anger she might have harbored for the way her eagerly awaited night turned out. "Why did you do it? Why leave a rose on my pillow in my bedchamber for me to find rather than attend the celebration as all in the lands expected? Why have me meet you alone and so far away on a mountaintop in the middle of the night?"

"There were reasons I shall share in time. Trust me to reveal them when the time is right."

She stared at him, watched the shadow move through his solemn expression, and nodded. She would wait. As long as she had him now, did the reasons truly matter? She thought not.

"Will you sing for me?" His finger grazed over her slightly parted lips and a sizzling thrill sped through her bloodstream. "You sang that night on the mountaintop while you waited for me. You have such a lovely voice. Had I not loved you already, the mere sound of your song would have taken my heart."

He had listened to her that night. For how long? How long had he stood in the shadows while she sang, while she slept, before coming to bring her to the castle? More unanswered questions that truly mattered not, she decided and reaching up, laced her fingers through the ebony hair at his temple as she started to sing.

She chose a song of love. Always of love. This one with lyrics that spoke of a woman and the excitement she felt, the true completion when she set eyes upon her handsome love. It was a song she could relate to and the lines poured from her heart as she stared into Bronwen's eyes, every emotion, and every word especially for him.

He led her in a slow swaying dance to the rhythm of her song, spinning her once and catching her hard against him as he drew her back, making her fumble the words on a laugh. He smiled and everything inside her sang along, the beauty of his lips curving just so in amusement at her, caressing her heart in a feeling like no other.

When she ended the song, he ended their steps, bending his head to cover her mouth with his. "Such a lovely mouth," he said against her lips. "Such a lovely tongue." He stroked that tongue with his own, a slow and gentle glide of warm flesh to flesh that had arousal sparking and needs screaming.

His hands moved up her sides and then down again to grip her hips. He lifted her effortlessly to her toes, changing the angle of the kiss to take it deeper, hungrier while keeping to the slow agonizing pace she had come to expect from him. Hormones raged, juices pumped, and her core ached. Only the smallest part of her mind managed to think around the quickly collecting sexual fog and it was that part she fought to grasp. Shoving her hands between their bodies, she gave his chest a light push as she drew away.

"Conversation before the fire requires our mouths to actually speak rather than taste and explore." She was breathless from the kiss and it took away some of the impact to her words. Or perhaps it added to the impact for him, knowing a mere kiss left her barely able to speak, to breathe.

He smiled again, a slow and devious tilt to his lips that had her belly tilting in much the say way. "We could allow our mouths to do all three."

She laughed, shook her head, and let her hand slide down to clasp his as she moved another step back. "For now, we concentrate on the first." She led him to the cover he spread on the floor and tugged him down with her as she lowered herself to sit. She reached for the closest goblet, needing to wet her throat after the soul stealing kiss, but stopped short and shot him a questioning glance when his hand grabbed her wrist.

"This one is for you, little one." He held out the other goblet while picking up the first for himself.

Calliope's gaze flicked to the goblet she now held. She saw her darkened reflection in the reddish-brown liquid that filled it, and then looked at Bronwen. For a single heartbeat, a trickle of fear wiggled down her spine and, for the first time since the night of her celebration, the spell crossed her thoughts. Why was Bronwen so intent she drink from this glass and not the other? Aithne had ingested a poison put in a goblet of wine much like this one when it had been her time between moons. Her sister had nearly died from that poison.

Stupid. She ruthlessly shoved the thought aside, stamped out the fear. There was no poison in this cup. The one Aithne took had all been part of the curse laid upon her. Calliope's part of the same curse spoke nothing of a death from the inside out as Aithne's had done. Hers spoke only of darkness and monsters. Though she had not been outside since arriving at the castle, with Bronwen and Reinn she had seen more sunshine than any that brightened the day. And Bronwen was no monster. The only of that kind she found thus far visited her in her nightmares.

To prove to herself she was indeed being silly, she lifted the goblet to her lips and took a very healthy sip. Red grape wine just as every other cup Bronwen served her when they were together this way. The flickering flames from the fireplace glistened off a carving in the side of the goblet and she turned it in her fingers for a better look. A carving of a man standing beside a large dog. On the opposite side of the goblet were the letters B and R.

"Why the man and his dog?" she asked, leveling her gaze on Bronwen. Would he give her the same answer she had gotten from Reinn when she found a similar painting during her cleanings? "Who is he and what is the significance?"

* * * *

"My father was a lover of animals." Bronwen sipped from his own goblet, let the wine move about his mouth, tasting the lace of blood it contained before he swallowed. It was true enough. His father had loved animals, though these particular goblets never belonged to his birth father.

"And the letters, B for Bronwen and R for Reinn?"

"Yes." And that was the complete truth. Randolph, the sire of the castle had the goblets made for his sons, at least that was how he came to think of Bronwen and Reinn over the decades. Since his death, the carving and letters now stood as an insignia of the new masters of the castle.

"But you are not brothers." Calliope angled her head, her eyes studying him.

"No, we are not brothers. We are," he hesitated, drank another sip to buy some time, "friends." That too was the truth, if not the whole of it. He and Reinn were friends and had been nearly since they first met. These days, however, they were so much more. How to tell her they were lovers, too? How would she react to know it was the three of them meant as one rather than three sets individually?

"Where is your family? Your father, what happened to him? I have seen no one else around but you and Reinn."

"They are not in this world." Likely dead by now, he thought as he stared at the fire. For humans do not live year, by century, by millennia like monsters. He saw shapes of them in the flames. His father so tall and virile, his mother so delicate and fragile, his sisters so young and beautiful. He had not thought of them in so many decades. Yet their pictures were as clear as yesterday in his mind.

Calliope gasped, shifted, and then touched his shoulder lightly with her free hand. "You were separated." Her words were barely a whisper. Without his heightened senses he might not have heard her. "When the door between worlds was closed forever, you were separated from your family."

Bronwen slowly turned his head to look at her and caught the glimmer of tears in her breathtaking eyes. Affection, understanding, and grief for him. It was better than pity, he decided. Pity is what he would see there if he told her the whole truth. Pity and fear.

"We were separated," he confirmed with a stiff nod.

"And Reinn? Is that what happened to him as well?"

"Reinn's story is a bit different from mine, but he too was separated from his family. In that way, at least, we are alike."

"I have heard stories, families torn apart by the wars of that time, people caught in a place not their own when the doors between all worlds were sealed. I cannot imagine it myself." She shook her head, her voice so full of disbelieving sorrow. "To stay behind while my family goes away for a time, thinking so certainly they will return, only to have their way home closed off for eternity."

She believed it had been them who left him. He would allow that belief to stand for now. To tell her it had been he who left, he who was not of this world, and the whys of his departure would only bring about more questions he cared not to answer.

"So much was changed when those doors were closed off, so many lives affected."

It was Bronwen's turn to study her now, her turn to gaze into the fire. "Your own family changed as well, your land and the future of its people, your future." He knew of the curse cast upon her, knew that for her sisters that curse had been broken by decisions they made regarding their true hearts. There was no decision for Calliope.

To be engulfed by a world of darkness to reside in terror and face a monster that will bring a death of no end. By his calculation, she was already halfway fulfilling that curse. By bringing her here to this castle to live with him and Reinn, he had fulfilled it in half himself. And the rest... He shuttered to think on that now.

"You speak of the spell." She did not turn to him but rather continued to stare at the fire. He wondered what she saw in the flames. The goddess queen and king, her sisters as he had seen his own? Or did she see a manifestation of her fears from the spell, her vision of the monster perhaps?

"I do not think it changed my future, really." Though her voice was not as confident as it had been, he decided not to comment on it. "I am where I was always meant to be." She finally looked at him and though there was a hint of fear in her eyes, he also saw a firm belief in what she spoke. "I am with who I was always meant to be with. We are paired by the guardians, coupled and set to meet our destined heart when the time is right. If there are tragedies to face, darkness to fall or monsters to battle, it is for us to fight together."

Oh, he wished she were right about that. Like so much that had been said between them this night, what she spoke was indeed a half truth. It was the whole truth that held the grave danger. Bronwen had no doubts they would face tragedies, darkness and even monsters together. But there was still the fact that he and Reinn were monsters as well. A death with no end...

"Perhaps the spell speaks of a different sort of monster than you picture," he suggested and drained his goblet of blood-laced wine. "Perhaps this monster cannot be pictured. Perhaps it is your destined heart that is the true monster."

She laughed, a sound of compete amusement and disbelief. Setting her goblet to the side, she shifted to her knees and walked on them to his side. "If you are a monster of any kind then I am the most powerful goddess of all worlds and lands."

Bronwen's lips twitched despite himself. Demigoddess that she was, he knew she held no powers whatsoever as a goddess. Her sisters held some. Or so he had heard. Both gaining a minute power when their parts of the spell were broken. The oldest daughter, Aithne, gained the power to heal and Karan, the middle daughter, the power of transport. Karan was, come to think of it, the only one in all the worlds with the power to move about freely and even she was limited to the number she could move with her.

What power would Calliope gain as part of her own spell? What limitations would it hold? When she fulfilled the curse upon her, would her power be that of immortality in darkness? As a demigoddess, she held part human blood. That part rendered her a certain level of mortality. It was the goddess blood of her mother and half-blood Fae of her father that caused her to age with such slowness that she merely seemed immortal. Still, he knew first hand that immortality in darkness was certainly no power gifted but purely more of a curse.

"Then I must be a monster because you truly hold a power to rival any goddess."

"Oh?" She hiked up the skirt of her dress to her thighs, swung a leg over his, and settled in his lap. "And how do you figure this?"

"Your eyes captivate me." He lifted a hand to her face and rubbed the pad of his thumb lightly under one eye. "It is them I see in the dark when I close my eyes. They light the way for me, give me hope until next I see you again. Your voice," he skimmed his thumb down to her mouth, traced the heart shape of her upper lip, "both speaking and singing, seduces me like no other. I hear it in my mind, feel it in my heart, my loins. Your heart," again he slid his hand down, this time splaying it between her breasts where her heartbeat at a steady excited tempo against his palm, "spreads such joy and life that I feel I would be nothing without you. It has consumed me, far beyond the charge of the guardians, beyond our destinies, beyond any idea of love I ever thought to know. That, my precious little one, is true power."

* * * *

The eyes he spoke of so poetically misted. The heart he extolled rose to lodge securely in her throat. Calliope stared at him through the blur of tears and knew absolutely nothing to say. She brought her hand to cover his between her breasts and leaned in, kissing first his forehead, his nose, and then finally his lips.

"I love you." Her voice cracked on the words.

"As I do you, Calliope. Always." His free hand snaked beneath her hair to cup her nape and he took the kiss from a light brush of lips to a deep and soul searching plunge.

Still holding his hand, she guided it to her breast and moaned softly into his mouth when that hand began to knead and caress. Despite her earlier desires to talk, to have her myriad questions answered, what she needed most now was his touch. She wanted his hands on her flesh, his mouth captured by hers, his cock inside her. Reaching between their bodies, she found his groin, and unlaced his breeches.

When she curled her fingers around his shaft, it was he who made the low moan into her mouth. With a finesse and skill she had not known she possessed, she pulled his cock free of his breeches and shifted on his lap until she felt the head rub over the outer flesh of her folds. Spreading her knees wider on either side of his hips, she lowered herself, taking him fully and completely inside her channel in one easy glide. Never once did she break the kiss.

"Mmm." As his lips moved from her mouth down her neck, she tipped her head back to expose more flesh for him to kiss, to lick. She held still on his cock, loving the feel of it buried to the hilt inside her core. Her muscles expanded around his girth, her channel seeming to stretch to accommodate his delicious length. She was wet, but not so much that she had not felt the gentle give and take of her body as she drew his cock inside her.

He pushed at the sleeves of her dress, inching down the bodice as he licked his way over her collarbone. When he freed her breasts, he immediately covered both with his hands, squeezing and weighing them in his palms, his thumbs and forefingers lightly rolling her taut and achy nipples until a fire blazed from that point in a direct line to her pussy.

Using her knees on the floor for leverage, she lifted herself off his cock, stopping only when she feared he might slip free, and then lowered herself once more. Though a part of her wished to ram his cock inside her as hard and fast as she could ride, she kept to his unhurried rhythm. This was Bronwen, her slow and delicate lover. It drove her mad to keep to that measured pace, the easing up and floating down, as his hands worked her breasts and his mouth explored her flesh.

Her body shook with the need for more, faster, harder. Still, she resisted. Her efforts had the orgasm creeping into her core, her juices flowing from her channel to soak their bodies where they met on the downward slide. She rocked her hips on that slide, a small gyration that ground her clit over the raspy hairs of his groin, and the orgasm grew claws.

"Bronwen." She was not sure if she said his name aloud but knew the cry that followed sounded in the silence of the great room as her muscles tensed, clamping around his cock as the claws of the orgasm dug into the sensitive walls of her core.

He bent lower, his licks finally making their way to one breast. He sucked her nipple between his teeth, rolled it there as he had done with his fingers before at the same moment that she took his cock deep, ground her clit on his body, and she lost it. Her body jerked, convulsing uncontrollably as the orgasm tore through her and she collapsed in his arms.

* * * *

Bronwen stood before the fire, staring into the dancing flames and this time it was Calliope's face he saw. He had taken her to bed, lain with her until she drifted to sleep, and then quietly rose and left as he did every night. It pained him to walk away. If he could have one wish granted at that very moment it would be for a single night to stay with her, to hold her until dawn broke across the sky. Perhaps he could have that wish, he mused, if he told her the truth. *When* he told her the truth.

"We cannot continue to keep secrets from her." He said it without turning around, without even looking behind him though he knew Reinn was there. He sensed his wolf, the faint smell of sweat from his nightly run in the forest, the traces of arousal that always built within Reinn after the adrenaline rush of the wolf, the returning change to man.

"Something has happened."

Though it was said as more statement than question, Bronwen answered. "I caught her heading out the front doors just after nightfall. She wished to go for a stroll around the grounds."

"She wouldn't if she knew what lay in wait out there."

Bronwen crossed his arms and shot a glance over his shoulder. Reinn had stopped at the chair to the left of the throw Bronwen had yet to pick up. He leaned against it casually, one leg hiked to drape over the arm, his fingers laced and held before his crotch. In this new moment another wish formed, this one to possess the talent for painting. Had he been able to do so, he would have created Reinn in that pose to stay forever in brilliant colors on a canvas to hang above his bed in his chamber.

Desire stirred, his cock growing hard, his balls tightening in anticipated response. Reinn's eyes gleamed, telling Bronwen he failed to hide his hormonal reaction. Then the corner of Reinn's lips inched up in a smile that was both mischievous and devious and Bronwen could not help the chuckle. He shook his head and turned back to the fire.

"Did you miss me, lover?"

"Always." Bronwen heard Reinn's boots hit the floor, the soles rapping softly on the stone as he stepped up behind him. Reinn's arms slid around his waist, pulling Bronwen close. "Did you enjoy your run?"

"Not as much as I would have liked."

Reinn's sigh had Bronwen closing his eyes, letting his head fall back to Reinn's shoulder. "They are still out there then."

"Aren't they always?" Reinn scoffed. "They pace the protected wall, looking for us to come out, searching for a way in. We are as much prisoner in our own castle as we would be with them."

"With them we would be dead," Bronwen reminded him, closing his hands over Reinn's at his waist. "We have made her prisoner, too."

"We knew we would when we brought her here."

"You mean when *I* brought her here. You tried to talk me out of it, to stop me."

"She is our destined. We both know that. I may have tried to stop you, but we both know one cannot prevent destiny. She is meant to be here just as she is meant for us."

"Take her outside in the light tomorrow, keep her by the castle walls, inside the protection and you should both be safe."

Reinn's arms tensed, his body growing stiff against Bronwen's. "Are you sure that's a good idea?"

"They already know she is here. If one of us does not take her out of this place soon she will decide to disobey my request and go out alone. We cannot keep her locked away in here for all eternity. If you are with her, you can keep her safe."

"You could do a better job of it." Reinn's lips brushed Bronwen's ear, then his face nuzzled at Bronwen's neck, an affectionate caress from the wolf never far below the surface of his being. "I wish you could be with us."

Bronwen felt all his previous desires meld into one mirroring Reinn's. "As do I, my wolf. I find myself more jealous of you than you could imagine."

"It seems that emotion is making the rounds as of late. You envy me my ability to walk in the sun, to share that light with our woman."

"And our woman to share that light with you." Bronwen turned in Reinn's arms. As the taller of the two, Bronwen guided Reinn's arms to his shoulders and laced his own around Reinn's waist.

"While I envy our woman her nights with you and you for your nights with her." He sneered. "The guardians have created one interesting triangle in the three of us."

"It is we who have created that triangle, lover. We have not created an arrangement that is meant nor can it remain."

"She never talks about her nights with you. Not her time spent in bed with you, in any case."

"Nor does she discuss with me her exploits with you."

"Exploits?" Reinn laughed and this time is was full of humored delight. He lifted his chin and brushed his smiling lips to Bronwen's. "What a creative name for our lovemaking."

"Fitting, I figured, as I know you. I am not sure why she has not said anything to either of us unless she fears angering us."

"She might. A woman like her does not generally have sex with two different men."

"She has gotten bolder since coming here." Bronwen thought of the way she had taken the initiative to climb onto his lap that evening, to free his cock from his breeches and ride him until his eyes bulged out of his head and his balls screamed in pleasured agony. "You had something to do with that, I assume."

Reinn shrugged but that mischievous grin tilted his lips once more. "Perhaps. But do you think her bold enough to accept both of us at once? To understand that not only are we both meant for her and she us, but we are meant to be as three?"

Bronwen released Reinn as he stepped back and turned to face the fire. "We cannot continue this charade. All these secrets, they are no good for any of us. If we are to tell her the truth about all, she must first trust both of us and accept us together."

"Then you don't intend to tell her about our, shall we call them, other sides as of yet?"

Bronwen shook his head. Tell her of the monsters within them? Had he not tried in a way already this night? Had she not laughed off the idea? "One step at a time. Take her for a stroll on the grounds tomorrow as I said. Tomorrow night I will come to her as always. Wait for us in my chamber. I will bring her there. We will not tell her of our...other sides, but we will explain our relationship and the will of the guardians."

"Will you be able to stand it?" Reinn's voice dropped to a low and seductive purr as Bronwen felt him step to his back once more. Reinn's fingers curled around Bronwen's bound hair and tugged until Bronwen's head fell back far enough to meet the wolf's heated gaze.

Arousal sparked in icy shards to slice at Bronwen's cock and balls. Hunger stirred, both for blood and flesh, for control and submission. The first time had been Reinn's wishes and Bronwen's tender way. Tonight the wolf would be in charge.

"How jealous will it make you if she allows us both to take her tomorrow night? How jealous will you be as you watch me fuck her?"

"How jealous will you be, wolf?" Bronwen turned the question on him, already knowing the answer for them both. "You resisted your feelings for her from the start, but you have come to love her as much as I. I can see that when you speak of her, when you speak of us."

"I didn't want to love her as much for it was you I always wanted."

"Yes, but it is both of us that you have now, both of us who will have you tomorrow night."

Excitement swirled into Reinn's eyes, feeding the beast and the desires of the man. "But for tonight, I will have you to myself."

Bronwen fought against Reinn's hold on his hair, not so much to hurt Reinn or himself for that matter, but to offer a bit of resistance, to add a bit of thrill to Reinn's power trip. He heard the low rumbling growl in Reinn's throat and knew it excited the man as much as the wolf. It excited Bronwen, too. He was gentle my nature, preferring romance to dominance, the prolonged pleasure to immediate gratification. Still, to be taken with the rough insistence of Reinn's temperament was a pleasure all its own.

"Have what you will, Reinn." He felt Reinn at his back fumbling with the ties of his breeches. His own remained untied from his time with Calliope and he reached for them now, pulled them down, letting them fall to his ankles, to save Reinn the trouble.

"Eager, are we?" There was satisfaction in Reinn's voice as his hands moved to Bronwen's hips. He pressed his hard, meaty cock against Bronwen's rear, pushing it between Bronwen's cheeks but not inside in his anus.

"Just being of assistance." Enjoying the game, Bronwen swayed, arched, grinding his ass to Reinn's cock, letting it slide up and down the crack of his ass until he felt the pre-cum leading from the head to warm the flesh, lubricate the entrance.

"Damn, Bronwen, even when I'm in control you drive me mad." Reinn's hand gripped harder on Bronwen's hips, holding him steady. "Get on your knees, vampire."

As Bronwen lowered to the floor, Reinn removed first his boots and then his breeches until he was fully naked. He situated himself on all fours, knowing the position would offer the shorter man easier entrance to his body.

Reinn wasted no time. Bronwen felt him sink to his knees behind him, Reinn's hands spreading his ass cheeks, the head of his cock brushing the outer rim of his anus, ready to plunge. He stroked the head of his cock around the opening, letting the pre-cum grease the tight ring of muscles, and then he thrust inside.

Delicious pain mixed with insurmountable pleasure and Bronwen bucked against it, hips flailing, hands attempting to dig into stone as Reinn pounded his thick cock in his tender anus. His fangs protruded, wishing for the taste of blood, for the tender flesh in which to sink as spasms racked his own cock, his balls swinging from the brisk fucking to slap at his shaft. It was a primal, animalistic mating he knew Reinn could never do with anyone not part beast like himself. Bronwen rode on the sheer bliss of it as enthusiastically as Reinn rode him. When they came it was as one, bodies shattering in fits and spurts, a loud and explosive contentment from vampire, from wolf, from men, from lovers.

Chapter Seven

Calliope awoke to an empty bed but for the single white rose atop the pillow next to her and the note beneath. Not Bronwen, her mind registered immediately, for Bronwen always left a red rose. Reinn then, she smiled as she sat up, and reached for the note.

Dress comfortably and coolly. Meet me on the back terrace and we shall spend the day strolling the castle grounds.

She nearly shouted with excitement. A day on the grounds. Yes! That was exactly what she needed. She threw off the covers and bounded out of bed to dress, unwilling to waste a single moment of sunshine.

Less than ten minutes later she found Reinn all but basking in that sunshine on the back veranda. Despite the heat, he wore his long golden locks down, several tendrils blowing lightly in the warm breeze. His chest was bare as it often was, she noted, and he wore the brown breeches and leather boots she had come to expect from him.

He must have heard her walk outside because he turned, a small smile slowly unfolding on his lips, his eyes glinting with that ever present naughtiness she had grown to love. It wound her up, that impishness and reckless disregard for anything but fun and pleasure, and her heart stumbled even as her belly filled with electrified ecstasy.

"Good morning." He stepped to her and held out a hand. "You look beautiful as always."

Calliope angled her head. Interesting, she mused as she put her hand in his offered one. Reinn did not usually go for the charming idle compliments. "Thank you. I might say the same about you."

He chuckled. "You might but then men are not generally described as beautiful."

"Handsome seems to stately a word for you. How about we settle on dangerous then?"

"Dangerous?" Reinn cocked a sexy brow. "Is that a word of beauty now?"

"I have quickly discovered it can be. Especially when I am thinking of you." She closed the distance between them and rose to her toes to kiss his lips. "Yes, danger in you is a beauty beyond measure." She stepped back. "Now, what adventure do you plan to show me today?"

Laughing again, he shook his head. "My lady, I'm growing to learn that you can be as full of adventure as I. For starters, we shall walk. It's a beautiful day, many flowers are in bloom. Do you like flowers?"

"I am a woman. Of course I like flowers." She beamed a smile at him and let her hand slide down his arm to lace her fingers with his as they started to walk. Grass as green as emeralds covered the castle grounds, speckled with the various flowers of which Reinn spoke. Trees scattered about the rolling land and in the distance she thought she could just make out the glistening blue of a pond or lake. Taking the lead, needing as much time in the glorious sun as she could manage, she walked him in the direction of that blue. "You spoke with Bronwen, I take it."

"I did." He swung their arms between them as they walked, reminding her of how she and her sisters played when they were young. "We often speak about a great many things."

Calliope tipped her head back and narrowed her eyes. "My sister, Karan, she has a lovely name to call someone after they make what she would consider such a piffy comment. What is that name?" She tapped a nail to her chin and pretended to think then held up that finger. "Oh yes, it would be smart ass."

"My ass is not the only part of me that is smart, my lady." He gave a stately bow toward her, nuzzling his face at her neck for a little nip at the tender flesh just below her ear before he pulled away, the corners of his lips twitching in his obvious effort to hold off a smile. "I have heard tale your sister is an odd creature for a demigoddess."

"Because she is strong of body, of mind, and of will." She stopped for a moment, tipping her head back again, this time to let her gaze travel up the trunk of an enormous willow tree. Vines of ivy wound around the base, stretching up to fade into the leaves of the canopy. "She would find great pleasure in the limbs of this tree. The thickness of the branches, the texture of the bark," she touched her palm to the trunk between the winds of ivy, "She would find it fabulous for carving and building."

"Man's chores." Reinn scoffed and tugged on her hand to pull her along.

"And cleaning a castle is not a woman's chores?" Calliope turned her gaze on him and lifted a brow.

"So your sister likes to build," he said quickly and made Calliope laugh. "Does her mate?"

"Eric designs." She considered for a moment and then nodded. "And builds too, I suppose. He is what they call in his world an architect. They have begun their own company in Otherworld, though I believe it is Karan who does much of the business matters. She does enjoy the running of things. Eric has his hands full with her."

"Have you been there? To Otherworld, has she taken you there with her powers of transport?"

"No." Calliope sighed and shook her head. Karan had told her much about it though, all the tall buildings higher than the palace of the goddess queen, the motorized moving vessels known as cars, the boxes called televisions with people in them pretending to be other people. "She is not able to take any with her from our world. Only she and Eric may travel by her power."

"But she can use it within this world."

Calliope nodded. "She can poof her way around our lands all she likes, take others with her as well, but only two bodies at a time. She cannot move anyone but herself and Eric between the worlds."

"Poof, huh?" He chuckled. "I like that name for it."

"Another of Karan's lovely terms."

"Do you miss them, your sisters, the queen and king?"

"Naturally I do." She missed conversations with her mother of feminine joys and future plans. She missed stories with her father, a tradition Karan enjoyed more often than she as they grew into women, but one Calliope had picked up since her sister left the palace to be with their joined mates. She longed for walks among the palace grounds, the sounds of the bird's song, the incessant chatter of the palace servants and guards, the nearly ever present sunshine that brightened every day, and the smooth clear black of night speckled with the silvery jewels of the many moons and even more stars. "They are my family. Before now, I have never been away for any true space of time."

She cast a quick glance at Reinn, caught the flash of sorrow in his too handsome features. "That does not mean I wish I had not come here." She rushed to assure him. "This is my place now, with you and Bronwen. This is where I am meant to be. But you know how it is, I am sure. Bronwen told me of how you came to be separated from your parents when the doors between the worlds were sealed."

Shock moved through the electric green depths of his eyes, quickly masked by something she could not quite name. "He did, did he? Exactly what did he say of it?"

"Simply that your parents were trapped in the otherworld and you here when the doors closed." There was more to it, she realized now, more that neither man was telling her. What? Why did they not wish to speak of it? "Will you tell me the rest?" she dared to ask.

"Someday. Let us not ruin this time together with sadness and past stories." He stopped, yanked her arm until she spun around, and slammed into his hard body, front to front, delicate curve for rigid angle. The shock was gone now, as was the indiscernible emotion, making room for the mischief and hormone searing heat.

"I would rather enjoy seeing you naked now." His lips brushed hers, his teeth nipping her bottom lip in a not so gentle bite. "I would rather see you wet, the water glistening off your smooth flesh, beading on your nipples." He shoved fingers through her hair, letting them fist around the strands to tug in the same not so gentle way as his bite. "Your hair slicked back and cascading down your gorgeous body to the tantalizing crack of your ass."

Clear thoughts fled in the rush of arousal that sprinted through her from roots to toes, branching off to tease every erogenous spot in between. Twin demons of lust and excitement came alive in her core. The sun was hot above them, the air rippled by a warm and crisp breeze and in the distance she could just make out the sound of bird's song.

They were in the open and yet it was private. Would anyone see if they became naked here? If they made love here? Was there anyone *to* see? When she found the idea excited her more, drawing from her center a light stream of creamy juices to coat her sex, she felt the heat rise to redden her neck and face.

"You're blushing." Reinn's lips kicked up in a grin. "Why do you blush, Calliope? My words should not shock you anymore, nor should my desires."

"Not your words or desires." She shook her head. "The place. We are outside. Or have you forgotten?" She looked around, a quiet, "Oh," escaping her lips. They had reached the water without her realizing. It was a pond, she saw now and she slowly turned in Reinn's arms to study it. Lilies speckled the astonishing greenish-blue surface of the water while flowers of sunny yellow, brilliant white, deep purples, and radiant pinks lined the crisp green grass around the edges. Another tall willow tree was but a stone's throw from the pond, its long wiry branches reaching out above the water to offer shade. It was positively gorgeous, she decided, the scene hampered only slightly by the enormous stone wall now within view surrounding the castle grounds and stretching as far as her eye could see.

"Why don't you take off your clothes? It is the perfect weather for a nice long swim." Reinn nipped at her earlobe as he whispered in her ear. "Go on. I will be right behind you."

The temptation was too much to ignore. She could already feel the cool smooth water gliding over her flesh before she even got out of her clothes. With no more thought to watching eyes, she removed her dress, carelessly kicking it aside and ran for the pond, diving in.

* * * *

Lucky for her the pond was deep, Reinn thought with an appreciative chuckle as he paused to watch Calliope. He would be a fool not to. The sensual sway of her naked and very tantalizing hips as she ran for the water, the gentle bounce of her tits as she dove, the long stems of shapely legs that seemed to take forever to disappear beneath the surface with the rest of her.

Funny, he thought as he kicked off his boots and went to work on the ties of his breeches. She was not all that tall and yet legs like hers seemed to go on for miles. He had not really noticed that before now. Perhaps he should take more care and time from now on instead of always being so eager to sink his cock inside her sweet heat. Maybe there was something to be said for the slow romantic way Bronwen preferred to take things after all.

His cock gave a quick jerk of protest as Calliope broke the surface of the pond, water raining down her hair, face and shoulders, her breasts floating in a sort of devious invitation. Then again, he reconsidered and yanked off his breeches. There was a lot more to be said for filling such an incredible body with a certain eager and decidedly rambunctious part of himself.

"Come in." She scooped her wet hair from her face and shot him a wide happy grin. He had a moment to think how she looked more contented as that moment than she had seemed since coming to the castle before she threw herself back, executing a back flip complete with wide spread legs offering a mouth-watering view of golden pubic curls and pink lips, then disappearing beneath the water only to reappear a half-second later laughing. "The water is fantastic!"

"Not as fantastic as the view." He made a mental note to thank Bronwen for the suggestion he take her out today as he took his time walking to the pond. He could feel eyes on him and not just Calliope's. They were out there. His keen predatory senses were on high alert and telling him all he needed to know, all he had already known. They would be watching, waiting, looking for a chance to get to them, to her. They would get nowhere near her, he vowed. He may have fallen in love with Bronwen first, may have accepted his destiny with Calliope simply because the guardians deemed it so, but she had reached more in him these last couple of weeks. Destiny or not, he had fallen curly blond hair over booted feet for her and nothing, absolutely no one would touch her. No one of course but himself and Bronwen.

"Come here and I will show you more than a view." She patted the surface of the water with her palm, her eyes closing until only a seductive slit remained for her to peer through.

Not so shy now, he thought even as he chuckled. Monstrous. He didn't care for thinking of the beast that lived inside him, the beast Bronwen was, all the others who watched on, or even the spell that hung over Calliope, but just now the word held an entirely different meaning. Watching her, he knew, gone was the bashful demigoddess and in her place was a vicious and thoroughly devious sex monster.

"Are you attempting to tease me, Calliope?" He stepped into the water, moving in slowly, loving the way her gaze had slid from his to travel down his body. The hunger that rose in her eyes was intense and satisfying. His already stiffening cock hardened more at the sight despite the chill of the pond. When a woman like her looked at a man like that he could feel nothing but a sizzling heat and a flaming need to take her. It was as simple as that.

"It was not my intention but as it appears to be working..." Her words trailed off as her gaze locked on his cock. The water was up to his mid-thigh now and he stopped, laughed when her gaze leapt back to his. She wiggled her brows. "It appears to be working very well, actually."

Reinn dove. Pushing himself off with his feet, he fell forward and lunged through the water toward her. She gave a startled yelp, spun around, and swam in the opposite direction. He had no problems catching her. He was faster, longer and had the advantage of knowing his full intentions. She shot a glance over her shoulder just before he reached her, let out another girlish squeal that had her gulping in water and attempted to feign left. Reinn wasn't fooled. He steered right, caught her slim waist in the bend of one arm and plucked her almost out of the water even as he spun her around.

Laughing, breathless and so aroused he saw stars, he covered her mouth with his, pushed a leg between her thighs to spread them, and thrust his cock in the sweet wet heat of her pussy.

Her body stiffened in his arms for one delicious moment as she moaned her surprise into his mouth. Then she locked her arms around his neck, legs around his waist, and relied on him to keep their heads above the water as she took his cock deeper in her slick channel. Her muscles were like a vise around his shaft. The pond water mixed with her erotic juices to wash them away nearly as quickly as they seeped from her body. It made his thrusts feel tight and rough, leaving just enough slickness behind to prevent true pain for either of them.

Reinn kicked his legs until he moved them closer to the bank of the pond where his feet could touch bottom. His hands moved beneath her butt, his fingers gripping her cheeks quite firmly as he allowed the need to piston his cock inside her channel in brisk and rapid succession to control him. Her nails raked the skin at his nape, the sting of the scrape offering another electrifying jolt of pleasure as the water crashed around them.

She wrenched her mouth from his, let her head fall back, and went all but limp in his arms as he fucked her hard, harder, hardest, drawing fabulous little whimpers of pleasure from her slightly parted lips. Her breasts bobbed as her body jerked and she looked so absolutely gorgeous at that moment he could do nothing but watch her in awed admiration and carnal lust as he continued to take her, to claim her, to make her his.

"You are so beautiful, so soft, and so hot." He curved one arm beneath her buttocks to support her weight, freeing his other arm to touch her. He danced his fingers from the tantalizing dip of her throat down through the valley between her breasts to her stomach. His gaze followed his finger, stopping only when his hand dipped below the waterline, wishing the water wasn't so deep so he could see his cock as it moved in her pussy.

"By the guardians, Calliope! Do you know what it feels like to be inside you?" He ground the words through clenched teeth as her hips rocked against him, her heels digging into his buttocks to hold him close, draw him deeper. "Your muscles close around my cock like teeth, biting and chewing until my balls tingle and tense with the need to come in you."

"Do it now, Reinn." Her head jerked up, her eyes glassy and unfocused. "Come in me now. Come with me now."

He did. With that stunning request, he drew his hips back and pistoned his cock inside her to the hilt, letting the ejaculation overcome him as her pussy convulsed around his shaft. Her body quivered in his arms, her head falling to rest on his shoulder as his cock drained in her channel. His muscles weak, knees knocking, breath ragged, he managed a quick, raspy warning. "We're going under." Then he gave into his body's need to relax and sank beneath the surface, taking her with him.

* * * *

"Do you believe in monsters?"

Reinn froze, a chunk of cheese in his hand headed for his mouth, his gaze snapping to her. Fear iced his veins, shock muddled his thoughts. Calliope sat across from him on the grass, her hair still a bit wet from their swim, her legs outstretched, her dress clinging seductively to every glorious curve. She reached for the goblet of wine they brought out for their impromptu picnic, sipped and eyed him over the rim.

It was the quick flash in her eyes that told him her question was not as casual as she wished him to believe. Still, why ask? Why now?

We cannot continue to keep secrets from her. Bronwen's words echoed through his mind. Then he remembered the morning he had gone to Calliope, found her so pale and shaken. A bad dream, she had said. *I do not wish to tell you. It was too ugly. I do not wish to remember it enough to put it to voice.* Did she somehow already know? Did she sense the truth?

"What kind of monsters?" he heard himself ask and forced himself to eat the bite of cheese, to sound and appear as casual as she attempted.

Calliope shrugged, sipped again, and sat the goblet carefully on a level patch of ground beside her. "Monsters. Any kind, I suppose. Do you believe in them?"

"I have had to." His gaze fell to the ground as he whispered words he truly had not meant to say. It was not the grass he saw but a vision of himself in wolf form, of Bronwen with fangs bared and blood lust in his handsome eyes. Even as the images disgusted Reinn, they aroused him. Then there was his father, the anger and contempt, the disgust and loathing. "There are many kinds of monsters," he said softly and shook off the vision and pulled his gaze back to hers. "Do you ask because of the spell? Are you frightened of what may still lay in wait for you to face?"

"You know of the spell." She sounded more resigned than surprised. "I suppose I should have known you would. Bronwen knows, after all. How?"

Confused by her question, Reinn wrinkled his brows. "How what?"

"How do you know? How does he know?"

"I know because of Bronwen but..." He broke off, thinking. How did Bronwen know? Had he ever actually said? "I guess he heard it somewhere."

"It is not talked about in our world. At least it was not before the trio of celebrations began. My sisters and I knew nothing of it until the night Aithne was set to meet her destined."

"It was hidden from you. To protect you. To prevent you from growing up in fear."

"I suppose. I am not afraid now," she said quickly and the defiant way she lifted her chin had him both wanting to laugh and nibble his way along her jawbone. "As I told Bronwen last night, neither you nor he are monsters of any kind and any I may face will be taken out." She gave a small laugh at that. "I am starting to sound like Karan now. She is the one always prepared to battle. But in this I shall be as well. I finally have all I ever dreamed, I have my destiny and I will fight what I must to keep it always."

Touched, torn, Reinn leaned over and caught her face in his palms. "You never cease to amaze me, Calliope." He brushed his lips to hers, thinking. They had only to tell her the truth and they could ease much of this fear she claimed not to feel. Tell her the truth and make her understand. She had already met the terms of the spell. She was already living a life with monsters. To a woman like Calliope, that would be a prison of a sort, residing in fear with two men who already lived a type of death with no end. But it didn't have to be a prison for her. They could show her she had nothing to fear from him and Bronwen. They could make her understand and they would begin tonight.

* * * *

Bronwen found Calliope standing before one of the ceiling to floor windows in the second floor parlor. He bit off the impulse to command her away from the window, to order her to close the heavy drapes. Safe here, he reminded himself. She was safe within the walls of the castle. Likely safe within the walls of the grounds as well, but he cared not to take chances there. If she went out it would be with either himself or Reinn as it had been today.

He was still several steps from her when she turned, a slow and radiant smile unfolding on her lips. Her skin was flush and he realized it was the sun she enjoyed that day that put the color to her cheeks, the light in her eyes. It pained him as much as it pleased him to see that light, that happiness and to know its source. It was something he could not give her, would never be able to share with her and for that, in that single flash of time, he envied Reinn more than he ever thought he could.

Was there anything he could give her that Reinn could not? Anything to even the score? Darkness and death, he thought with disgust. He could offer her only darkness and death just as the spell upon her predicted.

"I wondered when you would come to me." She walked to him, closing the distance between them in a few quick steps, and slid her hands up his front to his shoulders, wound her arms around his neck. "I missed you." Rising to her toes, she nipped his bottom lip with her teeth.

Bronwen moaned, curved an arm around her waist, drew her closer, and buried his nose in the top of her head. She even smelled of the sunlight, of the breeze from the day, of the flowers in bloom. "And I missed you, my love. Did you enjoy your day on the grounds?"

"I did." She pulled back and beamed a smile at him. "Oh, I did. Reinn and I made a picnic near the pond. We went for a swim and strolled the grounds. There is such beauty in the rolling land, so much area to explore. You should have been with us." Something moved through her face at that, a dimming switch to the excitement that animated her expression.

"I wish I could have been." He watched her, wondering what could have so suddenly stolen that happiness. Wanting it back, *needing* to see it despite the curl of envy in his gut, he asked, "So you went for a swim in the pond?"

Naked, no doubt. It was yet another experience he would not get to share with her, skinny dipping in the pond beneath the heat of the sun. Still, the mere image made his cock stiff.

"Why are you never with us?" She stared at him so imploringly he was certain if his heart had the power to beat, it would have stopped in that moment. "And why is he never with you and me?" She pulled away from him, shaking her head, and turning her back to him. She crossed her arms and shook her head again so quickly the long curtain of her silky hair swayed back and forth at her back.

"I cannot do this anymore. I cannot keep quiet, cannot keep my questions bottled inside." She whirled on him and the animation was back in her face but not with happiness. He saw confusion, torment and so much sadness it made his throat tight, his stomach churn.

"Calliope, little one, my love." When he reached for her, she backed away. Bronwen let his hand fall back to his sides, desperate to do something and unknowing what to do next. He had hurt her. *They* had hurt her. And it was only the beginning.

"I am having sex with Reinn, too." She said the words quickly, as if she needed to get them out before she choked. To his astonishment, she thrust her chin in the air and glared at him in such a way that defied, dared him to show any sort of disapproval.

Bronwen chuckled, and then stifled an even louder laugh when the sound brought a spark of anger to her incredible eyes. He stepped to her again, reached out and this time caught her before she could evade his embrace. "Do you think I do not know that?" He framed her face with his palms and tilted her head back. "Look at me, little one. Do you think I do not know you share yourself with Reinn in the day? That he does not know you are mine at night?"

"I...you...but you, neither of you have said anything."

The shock on her face mixed with the faintest twinge of pink made him smile. "Neither did you before now."

"I..." She faltered again, her gaze falling from his though he still held her face in his hands. "I did not understand at first and then I, well, I did not want to have to choose."

"Because you want us both? Because you feel for us both?" Bronwen kept his tone comforting, easy. She was terrified, he realized, of her own heart, her own desires, of how he would react, what he might think of her. "Is that it, Calliope?"

She nodded but did not speak, did not look up again.

"Close your eyes." He brushed his thumbs over her lids as they obediently closed. "Keep them shut and trust me. You do trust me, do you not?"

Again, she nodded, adding a barely audible, "Yes," but her eyes remained closed. She stood utterly still but for her breathing, even and slow as if she were almost afraid to move even that much.

Bronwen dropped his hands from her face to her waist, watched to be sure she continued to keep her eyes shut, and then drew her closer. He let his own eyes close as he reached inside himself and embraced his powers as intimately as he held her. A split second later, he opened his eyes and found Reinn staring at them, amusement and surprise warring for paramount expression in his dazzling eyes.

"I don't suppose it occurred to you to knock?" Reinn muttered but there was as much a smile in his voice as on his handsome lips.

Calliope's eyes flew open and she whirled in Bronwen's arms. She made a quiet gasp of surprise then shot Bronwen a look over her shoulder. "You have the powers of transport, too?"

"Only within our world. I cannot move between as your sister." And the power he really possessed was not that of transport but rather the ability to fly and move at lighting speeds. He kept that much to himself for now given that it was his nature as a vampire that gifted him with such power.

He glanced at Reinn, saw that he had been in the process of putting on a shirt when he and Calliope appeared. Muscles rippled in an enticing invitation for fingers, tongue, and teeth, all of which tingled with lust as Bronwen momentarily lost himself in the sight. Strange, he thought as his gaze slid up to Reinn's, how they lived together for centuries and he had always managed to control himself, the sexual urges to take, the desires to have and explore the other man until they brought Calliope into their lives.

Until *he* brought her here, he corrected himself, his gaze moving back to Calliope. Her attention was flicking back and forth from Reinn to him and back again though he had noticed the sight of Reinn's bare chest had given her as much pause at first as he.

"Calliope and I were about to have a conversation that concerns the three of us." He met Reinn's gaze over Calliope's bopping head. "I thought you might wish to be a part of it."

"You could have summoned me rather than appear in my bed chamber." The heat Bronwen felt in his own eyes was mirrored in Reinn's.

Bronwen bit back a smile. He knew why his wolf was all but growling over the fact that he had brought Calliope here. The enormous unmade bed beside him was only part of the reason. Reinn never was one for restraining himself against temptation. Except when it came to keeping his hands off him all these years, Bronwen mused and wondered how his friend had managed not to go insane. How had he not gone nuts himself?

"I could have," Bronwen said slowly. "But I did not see the point. I doubt there is any need for that," he told Reinn when he moved to put on the shirt he held.

"Oh?" Reinn lifted a brow, his gaze dropping to Calliope's before returning to Bronwen's. "I wonder if the two of you would mind telling me what I have missed."

"I am not choosing between the two of you." Calliope's briskly vowed words hit the air in the room like an enormous boulder falling from the sky. Reinn actually took a visible step back before his other eyebrow arched, amusingly joining the first.

Bronwen chuckled and moved his hands to Calliope's shoulders where he began to massage. "We are not asking you to, little one. As you can guess," he said to Reinn, "she has made it known that she is having sex with us both."

"Just not at the same time. Yet." Reinn said the last with a seductive hint that crawled over Bronwen's flesh, seeping in to rain through his body and harden his cock.

"The same happened to Aithne." Calliope stepped away from Bronwen, walked a few paces and then stopped, turning where she could see them both. "She had to choose between Hakan and Dustin, even though she felt for them both. I do not wish... What do you mean at the same time?"

Reinn's lips twitched as he moved to her. "It's about time you listened to us. Though I must say I do enjoy you when you're angry. She is so sexy with she gets a bit of temper going," he said to Bronwen.

"This I can see." Bronwen bit back a grin of his own as he too moved toward her until both men stood at her sides. "What he means, little one, is that we are all meant for one another. You know this. You have simply yet to admit it."

"I am your destined just as you are mine." Reinn snaked a hand beneath her hair and cupped her nape. "I will admit I had a problem with that at first. I didn't know it until the night of your celebration."

"You were angry that first morning. I sensed it in the way you were with me. You are always more insistent, rougher but that morning..."

"I nailed you, fucked you, and yes, I was angry."

"I am your destined too just as you are mine." Bronwen drew her attention to him by hooking a finger under her chin and turning her head. "I have always known and always wanted. But what you do not know, what neither of us realized fully was that Reinn and I are destined as well."

Chapter Eight

Calliope blinked at Bronwen. What was he trying to tell her? *Reinn and I are destined as well.* What did that mean? She slowly turned her head and found Reinn gazing down at her with a new intensity she had not seen before. In that moment, she understood. "You are lovers. The two of you are meant just as you are both meant for me."

Rather than answer, Reinn simply nodded. His fingers kneaded the muscles at the back of her neck as Bronwen's hands had messaged her shoulders only minutes before. Apparently they expected her to be filled with tension by their news. It almost made her laugh.

"How do you feel about that, little one?" Bronwen's question drew her attention back to him. She noted immediately the stiff set to his shoulders, the carefully blank expression, and the grim set to his lips. He was afraid, she realized. Her big, strong, and gentle lover was afraid of how she might react to the knowledge that he was also Reinn's lover.

"Lucky." The word was out of her mouth before she even thought to say it. When it drew a bark of laughter from Reinn, she turned back to him and felt the grin tugging at her own lips. It was the truth, she considered, however impulsive her response. Perhaps she had been innocent, shy, and naive when she came to live with these men, perhaps she was still on many levels, but it was not so much for her not to recognize what she had or to want what they were obviously offering her.

"You are okay with this?" Bronwen's voice was a combination of intense relief and complete wonder.

"I am more than okay with this." She turned to him once more, this time with her whole body and not just her head. Reinn's hand slid from her neck as she tipped her head back, her arms winding around Bronwen's shoulders. Reinn's fingers danced lightly down her spine until his hand finally settled on her waist. "I am more than okay with this," she said again and watched as her reassurance eased a miniscule amount of the fear in Bronwen's expression, felt it slowly seep out of his muscles. "I love you. I love Reinn." Because it felt as though she should, she reached a hand down to cover Reinn's on her waist. "You both love me."

"And we love one another," Reinn added and moved in at her back.

Sandwiched between them now, Calliope let her head fall back against Reinn's chest. Her fingers still around Bronwen's neck toyed with the hairs at his nape. "Show me." She loved the mixture of challenge and excitement she felt in Reinn just now, found herself equally amused by the trepidation and eagerness she felt from Bronwen. "Show me how much you love me. Show me what it will be like for us to be three."

She saw their gazes meet, felt Bronwen's slight nod, watched as the devious grin she found so incredibly sexy and thrilling unfolded on Reinn's lips. Both of his hands were on her waist now and he moved closer still until she felt his rigid erection in her lower back. He dipped his head, brushed a kiss to her nose before capturing her mouth in a kiss that was demanding and possessive and so hot she wondered the air did not sizzle around them. When he wrenched his mouth from hers, she gasped in protest and sheer satisfaction, in a plea for more and thanks for the toe-curling arousal.

Her vision went blurry for an instant as her hormones leveled. Then she watched in a sort of awed anticipation, her hormones spiking to an all knew high as Rein leaned over her shoulder to capture Bronwen's mouth much in the same way he had detained her own. The kiss the men shared was savage and reckless, a carnal exploration of tongues and teeth that fed her building hunger. Needs curled inside her as fire ignited in her core. Her nipples beaded against Bronwen's chest, her hips swaying absently in Rein's arms, grinding her body against his stiff cock.

It was Bronwen who finally broke their kiss only to immediately bend his head to hers, to crush his lips to hers in a kiss more ravishing than any he had ever given her. He tasted of the ever present coppery sweetness she had grown to expect from his kiss and the hot, primal taste she had come to know from Reinn. Combined, the tastes drove her to a point just short of madness. Who would have thought seeing two men together, seeing *her* men together and having them both wrapped around her like unmovable walls would be such an incredible turn-on?

"You are still okay with this?" Bronwen asked against her lips. She felt him reeling in his control and almost wished he would not. It was not often that her tender, slow Bronwen lost himself so completely. Except, was that not what she loved about him?

She framed his face in her hands and met his gaze, not wanting there to be any doubt or misunderstandings. "I am more than okay with this. Watching the two of you," she let her grin unfold on her lips so wide she figured she looked like a giddy fool, "is more amazing than anything I could have dreamed."

"How about being with the two of us?" Reinn's hands inched down her hips to her thighs. He began fisting the material of her gown, bunching it up until she felt the chill of his leather breeches on the bare flesh of her ass.

Enjoying his obviously playful mood, Calliope shot him a look even as she wiggled her ass against him. The electric green of his eyes darkened with arousal as he gave a low growl of tormented appreciation. "I do not know yet. How about you show me?"

Reinn's mouth came down on hers once more, his tongue plunging between her lips in a vicious thrust of control and rapt hunger. His hands let go of the fabric of her gown to move to her body, one splaying over her butt cheek while the other pushed between her body and Bronwen's to find the soft patch of her pubic hair. Bronwen's knees bent in front of her, his groin pressing Reinn's hand to her middle and she realized Reinn was somehow managing to tease the bulge of Bronwen's cock even as he delved a finger between the slick folds of her pussy.

Juices flowed, pinpoints of pleasure ignited, and Calliope's fingers twisted in Bronwen's hair. Reinn lightly scraped a nail over her sensitized clit and she groaned her surprise into his mouth, his tongue taking hers on a wild dance of power and passion. Dimly, she felt Bronwen's head tug against the grip of her fingers. His head bent into hers and Reinn's and he licked a long, narrow path from her neck to her jaw. Reinn pulled back a fraction of an inch and then Bronwen's tongue joined theirs.

It was exquisite, a mind-altering fascination that left her so crazed she could not differentiate one sensation from the next. Their tastes combined on her tongue, one silky sweet, the other white-hot and demanding. Between her thighs, Reinn's finger pushed inside her folds, dipped into her opening and drew a low cry from her as he wiggled, curved, and pistoned into her core. Hands moved to her ass and again she dimly registered Bronwen's move. His palms cupped her cheeks, holding her hard and steady against his body, with Reinn's hand still between them, still fingering her, and still rubbing at Bronwen's cock.

It was Reinn who broke the kiss this time, expelling a quietly rumbling, "Ah, yes," as he drew back, eyes closed and an expression of total pleasure on his handsome face.

Calliope realized Bronwen had turned one hand into Reinn and was fondling the other man's cock through the leather of his breeches. Reinn's finger stilled inside her pussy, but she was too mesmerized by the sight of his pleasure, the feel of Bronwen stroking him against her rear that she did not think to protest. She wanted to watch and started to tell them so, but before she could utter a word, Reinn pulled his finger free of her opening and stepped back far enough she no longer felt the heat radiating from his body.

"Undress for us, my lady." The order sounded strained, as if he were fighting for control. It was unusual for him to fight it. Reinn was always the one to simply go with his body's urges. Take what he wanted and do it fast, rough, hard, dominating and thoroughly satisfying.

Though she thought to question, even to tease, she held her tongue and removed her gown as he told her. While she did so, she watched with undisguised lust as Bronwen moved away from her and began to strip. Their gazes met and he smiled. It was a warm curve of succulent lips, knowing and seductive, and she felt its effects all the way to her toes.

"Our lover will have more patience if we allow him a quick release first." Bronwen spoke softly but not so low that Reinn could not likely hear him from his spot close behind her. He touched her lightly on the arm as he moved by her, leaving a tingle of fire that caught like a spark to fuel and traveled straight to her core. "Come to me, little one."

Calliope turned to find Bronwen had crawled onto the bed and positioned himself in the center, his back leaning against the headboard. His legs were outstretched and spread wide, his cock long and hard against his flat stomach. He patted the bed between his legs, his eyes heavy lidded now from anticipation and intent.

Calliope shot a quick glance at Reinn. He stood statue still, naked now but for the expression of unabashed want on his face. Boldly, she stepped to him, traced the outline of his slightly parted lips with her tongue, and lightly trailed the tip of a fingernail down the length of his rigid shaft. She bit back a grin when his dick gave an involuntary jump at the touch.

"I believe you are about to be satisfied, lover," she told him in a deliberately seductive purr. "At least for a time."

Battling the urge to giggle at the low growl that rumbled from his throat, she moved to the bed. Bronwen watched her, the smile blooming into a full and stunningly handsome grin of amusement at her teasing byplay with Reinn. The grin morphed into one of utter torment and unadulterated need a half a heartbeat later as she dropped to her hands and knees and started to crawl from the foot of the bed to the spot he indicated between his legs.

Purposely turning the teasing on him, she let her gaze do a slow glide from his eyes down his body to his groin. She licked her lips, a slow and pointed slide of her tongue that drove her senses of taste as wild as it no doubt did his senses of feel.

"You have become quite bold since coming here, little one." Bronwen reached for her, one hand lacing through her hair, fisting.

"Tell me about it." Reinn's muttered oath had Bronwen's lips twitching.

"Have I become too bold for your taste?" Calliope leaned in, enjoying the low sizzle of pain that fizzled through her at the slight pull of her hair. She bit Bronwen's lip harder than she normally would and reveled in the way his entire body flinched from the light jolt.

"No." The word was a breathless whisper. "I want you to always say what is on your mind, to ask for what you desire, to tell us what you wish most. Now, turn and sit between my legs. I wish to test that newfound boldness, little one, as well as our lover's control."

She was not sure she understood but she turned anyway and settled herself between his legs. He caught her shoulders and pulled her back to lean against him, his hands skimming down her front, over her breasts and then reaching further to her thighs.

"Open for me, for Reinn. Let him see the glorious treasure you hide between these lovely thighs." His hands pushed her thighs apart, spreading her legs and drawing them up until her pussy was opened wide and fully exposed.

* * * *

"Is that not an amazing sight?"

Reinn didn't look at Bronwen but kept his gaze transfixed on the amazing sight the vampire spoke of instead. "Beautiful." He moved to the foot of the bed, the better to view the spread pussy exposed for his perusal. Light sunny pubic hair curled over delectable pale pink lips that glistened with a creamy white moisture he knew would taste out of this world. He watched a narrow stream of that cream leak from her channel, saw the muscles of her opening flex as if in invitation, and marveled at the magnificent swollen nub of her clit.

"It is yours, lover. Do with it now as you wish."

Reinn's gaze flicked to Bronwen's, then to Calliope's as he climbed onto the bed. "Bold as she has become, there is still a hint of innocence in our woman," he said to Bronwen. His hands burning to touch, he placed them on the underside of her legs and pushed them down, over Bronwen's hands where they held her behind the knees, to her buttocks. "She blushes when you hold her this way. When I look at her so open for me, so ready for my cock. Are you ready for my cock, Calliope?"

"Yes. I am ready, Reinn. Please."

Reinn closed his eyes and let the growl that curled in his throat come. His beast was alive tonight, pacing in the dark recesses of his body, looking for release, for a moment to run and play. He couldn't let it loose. That he knew without doubt for in wolf form he could hardly control the hungers that drove him. Hungers far too strong in the presence of Calliope for him to forget his need to hold back. He would have let go if it had only been Bronwen in the room but it wasn't. He couldn't.

"Do you know what that does to me? To hear you beg for my cock?" He opened his eyes slowly but it was Bronwen's gaze he met first and what he saw in their ebony depths was complete and utter understanding. Blood lust twisted in his gut, mixing with his predatory need for dominance.

"Please, Reinn." Calliope's voice dropped to that seductive purr that drove him crazy. With the pink flush of her skin turning redder by the moment, she reached between her legs and traced the outer edge of her pussy lip with her fingers. "I want your cock inside me, Reinn. Fuck me. Please, Reinn."

Bronwen chuckled. "Perhaps you should give the lady what she wishes, lover."

"Oh, I intend to." Reinn shuffled further between Bronwen's legs, between Calliope's. "And what are your plans?"

"To watch, my w—woman," Bronwen recovered quickly. He had nearly called Reinn his wolf as he so often did when they were alone. "To watch our woman as she takes your cock inside her. It will no doubt be a wonderful sight to behold."

Reinn wrapped his fingers around his shaft, positioned it at the opening of her channel, and plunged. Pleasure, exquisite, body-rocking bliss, shot through him at that first initial thrust and had him stopping inside her channel buried to the hilt and unable to move while the sensations rained through him. After several quivering moments, he began to move, brisk, hard plunges and quick, long retreats that had her body jerking in response, delicious pleasurable screams tearing from her sweet throat.

Her hands found his torso, nails biting into flesh as he drove himself more deeply in her than he'd ever been able to before. With her legs held high in Bronwen's hands, she took his cock with an ease and depth that shattered any semblance of human control he managed to hold and, beneath that, he felt the slippery grip on his beast start to give.

"Look at that, Calliope," Bronwen said softly over their pants and moans. "See how his cock disappears inside your body. Ah, little one, it is so fantastic."

Calliope's head lifted and for a moment they all three watched as Reinn fucked her, slamming inside her in measured thrusts. Her inner muscles contracted, fisted around his shaft and he threw back his head on a loud grunt.

"Gods, Calliope, loosen up. Your pussy is so tight, so wet and hot, so..." He lifted his head and met Bronwen's gaze once more.

"Kiss him." Calliope's breathless words took a moment to penetrate the combination of beastly desires and carnal hunger in his mind, his body, his soul. "Kiss Bronwen while you take me, while you fuck me. I want to watch the two of you."

Reinn shifted, leaning to the side of her, one hand on the bed to support his weight while he reached for Bronwen with the other. Just before his mouth closed over Bronwen's, he caught the glint of red beginning to pool on the tip of his tongue. Their faces were close enough, the angle just right that Calliope would not see the blood, but Reinn did as Bronwen no doubt intended. The vampire knew the blood lust curling in Reinn's veins and had bitten his tongue to share a bit of the blood he had consumed upon waking in an effort to offer some satisfaction to that single need, even as Calliope's body satisfied all of the others.

As their lips touched, Bronwen's tongue thrust deep, and Reinn lapped at it, drawing at the tiny droplets of blood that flowed from the vein Bronwen's fangs punctured and sucking out more. It was exquisite, the taste of the blood Bronwen shared while his cock rocked so deeply in Calliope's pussy. Her nails dug deeper, drawing more blood, this at his sides, and the pain, the pleasure, the tastes and sounds pushed him over the edge. He thrashed, tongue still tangling with Bronwen's, cock still plunging in Calliope's channel, his hips bucked faster and faster until the release exploded from the head of his dick. Dimly, he heard Calliope's answering screams as she came around him, her body jerking, juices coating his shaft as her body went limp between him and Bronwen.

* * * *

"I nearly let it slip." Bronwen spoke softly as not to wake Calliope. She lay between him and Reinn, her head on his shoulder, her hand holding fast to Reinn's arm draped over her waist.

"You recovered quickly enough. She didn't notice." Reinn raised his upper body, careful not to jostle the bed and wake Calliope. He rested his temple on one balled fist and eyed Bronwen. "How long do we keep it from her? We've come this far…"

"It is too soon tonight." Bronwen idly caressed her shoulder as he stared down at her. So peaceful in sleep, he thought. So sated after their love making, so beautiful, so sexy he wanted her again. "She only tonight accepted us together, the three of us. To ask her to accept all else," he shook his head, "it is too soon yet."

"She has nightmares. Did you know that?"

Bronwen stiffened, his hand freezing on her arm. He had not known. "What sort of nightmares?"

"She hasn't told me." Reinn sighed. "Pretty bad ones, if I were to venture a guess. I walked in on her early one morning, just after rising. She was pale, frightened. She claimed she had a bad dream, but she wouldn't tell me more about it."

"Do you think she senses it?"

"Senses us, you mean? Perhaps. Or it may simply be her fears of the spell, of the monsters manifesting in her dreams."

"Are we not the monsters of the spell?" Bronwen asked in disgust.

"Oh, we are monsters, no doubt. But we may or may not be the ones she fears most."

"We will keep her safe, Reinn. No matter what we must do, we will keep her safe."

Reinn nodded and leaned in to brush his lips to her bare shoulder in a tender kiss completely uncharacteristic to his nature. "Of course." He closed his eyes and took a deep, audible breath. "I never thought to care for her this way, to love her as much as I do you. How is it that I can have her, take her body and it never be enough?"

Bronwen smiled wryly. "I know the feeling as well. I can never seem to get enough of either of you."

Reinn looked up at him, his green eyes glinting in the darkness of the chamber. "Shall we wake her?"

Bronwen chuckled, shook his head, and felt the answer stiffen his cock. "And show her the advantages of two lovers at once? I think it is time for that."

* * * *

Calliope awoke slowly, eased out of sleep by gentle hands on her breasts, between her legs, tender mouths to her inner thigh, her neck and chest. A sliver of alarm raced through her at the sharp graze to the top of one breast. Memories of the nightmares, of the monsters and the horrid way such pleasurable sexual acts turned threatening and awful brought her the last few unconscious inches from sleep in a gasping rush.

"Shh, it is only us, little one." Bronwen's voice was soft, consoling, his hands as smooth and soft as velvet to her flesh as he worked to calm her.

"Do you want us to stop?" Reinn's breath was a warm tingling presence against the sensitive folds of her pussy.

Calliope blinked, the last remnants of the fear, of sleep fading in the presence of their assuring words and arousing touches. "No. Wow! What a way to awaken."

Reinn chuckled, quick burst of his warm breath sending slivers of burning embers shooting through her core. "You're wet." His tongue delved between her folds, licked her clit, and plunged inside her channel. She gasped, writhed and gripped for something to hold on to. Her fingers curled around Bronwen's shoulder. Reinn drew back smacking his lips and making an, "Mmm," sound. "And so very tasty."

"Reinn, you are teasing our lover." Bronwen's eyes glinted with a mischief she was accustomed to seeing on Reinn's face as he looked down at her.

"It's hard not to with a pussy like this." Reinn buried his face between her legs, drove his tongue inside her opening and wiggled, licked, fucked until she was thrashing in Bronwen's arms, panting and teetering on the verge of climax.

"It is my turn to enjoy that wonderful treasure. You must learn to share." Though Bronwen's words were scolding, the tone in which he said them held total amusement.

Reinn pulled back. "Oh, all right." He sounded like a child being told he had to give up his favorite toy.

Calliope extended her leg and curled it around Reinn's neck in a lightning fast move that actually drew a startled chuckle from him. "You two are very funny in the wee hours of night. I do not suppose I get a say in this." She was still panting, her body humming in crazed need for the release that Reinn left her a lick and a plunge from achieving.

"Do you wish him to continue, little one?"

She hurt Bronwen's feelings without meaning to. He wished to pleasure her and she was not allowing Reinn to move, to be replaced by her tendered, sweet lover. "What I wish is to come." That bluntness earned her a bark of laughter from Reinn and a smile twitching in the corner of Bronwen's lips. "You cannot awaken me with such erotic touches, bring me but a hairs breath from coming and then pull away!"

"Now who is looking for immediate gratification?" Reinn's hands skimmed up her thighs, over her folds, and slipped under her buttocks. "I thought I was the one who enjoyed the quick approach."

"I suppose I have learned from the master then."

Reinn bit the inside of his cheek and gazed at her considering. "Master? I believe I like that."

Bronwen closed his eyes and shook his head. "Now you have done it, little one." He shifted, stretched on the bed beside her, and reached for her. "Come to me, Calliope, and I will give you the penetration you crave."

She did not need to be asked twice. She rolled on top of him, straddling his waist, her arms on either side of his head. In one easy move, she lowered her hips and took his long, thick cock inside her sodden opening all the way to the hilt. She could not say for sure who moaned the loudest for all three of them made echoing sounds of pleasure and appreciation at the first sweet invasion.

Even Reinn was unable to keep quiet from his position at the foot of the bed. "By the Gods, that's a more amazing sight than watching my cock go inside her when I was on top. You should see this, Bronwen. The way her pussy opens to take you in. The sheen of creamy white her pussy leaves behind to coat your cock as she lifts away."

She felt the breeze first, a tantalizing mix of cool and warm over her sensitized flesh just before the satiny swipe of his tongue. Reinn leaned in and was licking her pussy and Bronwen's cock as she rode Bronwen, lapping at their mixed juices as Bronwen's cock eased out of her. The realization had her throwing her head back, a quiet, "Oh, wow," escaping her throat on a ragged breath. A breath that caught in her chest a moment later when Reinn's tongue moved over the tight rim of her anus.

"Reinn." She could not say if she meant his name to be warning, question, or plea. Her body stilled with Bronwen's cock lodged deep inside her channel, her muscles tensing in every limb.

"Ah." The sound was wrenched from Bronwen's lips. "She goes tight around my dick when you do that, lover. Does it excite you, little one? Do you like the way he tastes that secret part of you?"

"I…I do not know." It was the truth. She was not sure if she liked it or feared it most.

"I've tasted you here before, Calliope. You liked it then. I know you did. What I truly want is to enter you here." His tongue was replaced by a finger, the tip tracing the outer rim of the tight opening.

The breath she was holding blew out of a whoosh as his finger eased inside, pushing past the taut rim of muscles just inside, and wiggling slightly. She felt her anus stretching, the muscles giving for his probing finger.

"You would like it too. You do like it, don't you, Calliope? You like the way I finger you here?"

She could not answer, not with words anyway. There was little breath in her body for sound. Instead she nodded and felt the heat creep over her. No breath needed to blush. Her eyes were tightly shut, all her focus on that finger, on the odd sensation of pleasurable pain slithering through her. Then he pulled the finger away, only to push it in again, this time with a companion. Two fingers probed her anus, circled and stretched the tender tissue. Inside her pussy, Bronwen flexed his cock and she moaned at the intense awareness of having both holes pleasured at once.

"He is right. You do like that." Bronwen's voice sounded of both pleasure and heated amazement. "He does not wish to stop at the fingers, Calliope. Will you allow him to fill you there, to fuck you as he wishes?"

"You are so very responsive here." Reinn caressed her butt cheek with his free hand as his fingers continued to play in her secret opening. His touch was tender, almost sweet, as was his voice, two uncharacteristic traits for him that surprised her as much as they comforted. But it was the underlying heat of pure male arousal that crazed her most. He was enjoying himself and she wanted nothing more than to make her men happy. "Your body is saying yes. Feel how easy my fingers are going inside you now? Even with the loss of space to accommodate Bronwen's cock in your pussy, your ass is still spreading for me."

"Look at me. Calliope, open your eyes." She did and found Bronwen gazing up at her with so much tenderness it nearly brought tears to her eyes. All the love he felt for her was right there in his expression, all the love Reinn possessed for her right there in his tone, in his touch. "He will not do it if you do not wish it."

"Just say no, Calliope. That's all you have to say, my love."

She could not find the breath to say anything. When she remained silent, Reinn eased his fingers out of her anus and only then did she find her voice. "No!"

"Okay, okay." Both of Reinn's hands were on her butt cheeks now, skimming lightly over them, caressing and soothing. "No problem. We won't do it then."

"No!" Calliope shook her head, the movement almost violent as the absence of the penetration in her ass had emptiness coursing through her in a vicious wave. "That is not what I meant. Do not pull away. I want it, Reinn. I want you to fuck me there."

"Oh, Calliope." He growled the words as his hands stilled on her ass. "You have no idea what those words just did to me, my love."

Slowly, she looked over her shoulder, a smile unfolding on her lips. "Then show me, my love." Her use of his name for her had as much impact on him as her words. She saw it in the softening of his electric green eyes, the easy curve of his lips.

He nodded and moved into position. "Relax and I will show you."

She took a deep breath as she turned her head back and met Bronwen's pleased gaze. Reinn entered her ass slowly, both men moving their bodies when necessary to allow Reinn's cock easier passage with Bronwen's dick lodged deeply inside her vagina. The pressure was maddening, the pain-laced pleasure pulling a long musical moan from her as her body filled with the two incredible engorged cocks.

"Are you okay?" Reinn's concern was another kind of pleasure, the knowledge that he was restraining himself, holding his so often fragile control another form of satisfaction.

"Yes." She was better than okay. She felt fantastic!

"Stay still. Allow us to do the work." Bronwen's hands held her sides, Reinn's gripping her hips as both men held her still.

It was Reinn who set the pace, surprisingly measured strokes into her ass that were not too fast, nor too slow. As he thrust inside her, it rocked her body down and Bronwen continued the move, raising his hips to bury his cock inside her vagina, the base of his body rubbing against her clit.

She exploded. Without warning, the orgasm crashed through her, gushing out of her on a strangled cry that racked her body with spasms and convulsions, controlling her muscles and blurring her vision in a wash of white-hot light. Somewhere in the deep recesses of her awareness, she heard her men groan and growl as they too found release.

Chapter Nine

Reinn settled back on the warm grass just off the back veranda and watched in a sort of awed fascination as Calliope picked flowers, chased butterflies, and sang with birds. She reminded him of the princesses in the mortal fairytales his mother told his sisters as children. He'd thought them stupid, girly stories then. Watching Calliope, he saw the beauty of them now.

He couldn't keep her inside. Since their first outing barely a week before, he found it impossible to detain her within the palace walls in the day. He managed once, yesterday when clouds filled the sky and rain poured in sheets of darkness and gloom. For the first time in recent memory, Bronwen had risen early and been able to spend much of the day as well as the night by their side. Today, however, the sun shone bright once more, the plants and flowers revived by the nourishing wetness, the wildlife alive with the first promises of the approaching fall.

An audible gasp had him bolting upright, the beast inside him stirring to pounce. Hardly three feet away Calliope had fallen to her hands and knees, her head bent and shoulders shaking. Only when she lifted her head and he saw the wide grin spreading her lips did he realize she was laughing. It was contagious. An echoing smile unfolded on his face as he cocked his head to study her. She scooped her hair out of her face, flipped her body over, and rolled in the grass laughing like a loon.

"What in the..." Reinn muttered and shook his head. He started to get to his feet when she pushed to her hands and knees once more and crawled toward him.

Her hair fell on either side of her face, the ends nearly brushing the ground. Her dress bunched at her knees, scrapping the grass and likely staining the fabric with more grime and dirt than they would ever get clean. But it was her face, the wildly predatory gleam in her eyes mixing with the cheerful flush to her cheeks and the crazed smirk on her luscious lips, that had his cock growing stiff and the hunger awakening in his gut. In that position, on her hands and knees as she was, the beast inside him deemed her the perfect female for both mating and food.

"Is there a particular reason you are crawling on the ground?"

"I fell." She threw back her head and laughed at herself. "Did you not see the rabbit? I thought I would chase him, to catch him and play. He got away."

"And you hit the ground." Reinn chuckled despite himself. "Aren't you a bit old to be chasing rabbits?"

"One is never too old for such recreation." She said it almost primly, the regal tone of the demigoddess within her making a rare appearance as she stopped at his feet and settled on her rump. "You should try it sometime. A little fun could do you good."

"I have enough fun watching you." And he did. She was an absolute joy to behold. In less than three weeks time she had brought more life and fun into his world than he'd known in many millennia.

She sat with her knees bent, her arms around her legs hugging them to her chest. Thoughtfully, she plucked a blade of grass from the ground at his booted feet and began sliding it through her fingers. "I want to invite my sisters for a visit."

Reinn stilled and actually felt the color drain from his face, the smile faded from his lips. He looked away, needing to gather his thoughts before he spoke and unable to do so while staring at Calliope's brightly happy face. "You should talk with Bronwen first."

"I will, of course. I thought to talk with him tonight. You think he will have an objection to my sisters coming here?"

Objection was putting it mildly. It was too soon for anyone to come here let alone her sisters. But how to tell Calliope that? "Perhaps you could go visit them instead." He wasn't sure how Bronwen would feel about that suggestion or even how they would protect her if she left the grounds, but surely her going would serve better than two mere innocent demigoddess souls on such tainted ground. He looked at her, saw the confusion and disappointment erasing the happiness of moments before, but didn't know what to do about it.

They had not yet told her the full truth, had not yet revealed the other parts of themselves, the beasts within them to her. It was Bronwen's call. Reinn couldn't say exactly why—perhaps he was a coward or maybe it was simple fear no matter how uncharacteristic both were to his personality—but he left the time frame to Bronwen, the decision making of what was best for Calliope and when.

"I miss them, Reinn." Tears glimmered in her eyes and his heart twisted. Neither of them had ever wished to cause her pain, only to keep her safe. They could not do one without the other, he realized with a deep regret. "And I want to show my new home to them. There is so much to talk about, to plan."

Reinn narrowed his eyes, a sudden weariness moving through him. "What is there to plan?"

"Our joining, of course. The wedding. It will be a bit odd, I suppose." She gave a watery laugh. "I have never seen a joining between three people before but since it is obviously the will of the guardians, the destiny of each of us, then it shall be done."

"The wedding," Reinn repeated and the weariness morphed into a sudden all-consuming dart of sheer terror.

"The final phase of the spell is nearing its end. Only a little over a week until the days before the next new moon. I have to believe whatever horrors in which the spell spoke will come to pass before then. Unless it was wrong all along." She waved a hand in the air dismissively. "I do not wish to think on that now. Our wedding, that is what I want to discuss." Her reddened eyes glinted and a hint of an amused smile showed on her lips. "Does the thought scare you? I have heard it does some men, the idea of being joined with a woman. I do not understand why it would though as you already know and have accepted that we are destined mates."

He didn't know why it would either, why it did. Maybe it was simply because he had resigned himself to the fact long ago that he would never join with anyone. Not a woman, in any case. He had harbored hope for centuries that he would one day belong to Bronwen in some intimate way.

Reinn reached for her. She came into his arms without question and settled in his lap. "It scares me some." The admission surprised her. He saw that much in the sudden and slight drop of her jaw. "But it pleases me more, gives me a happiness I never thought to find. We will talk with Bronwen tonight, I will talk with him. There are," he hesitated, pushed a stray strand of her golden hair behind her ear, "things you still need to be told."

"What things? And why do you speak so grimly of them?"

"Tonight, my lady. You will understand tonight." Reinn silenced any further questions with a kiss.

* * * *

Bronwen sensed more than saw Reinn enter his chamber on the lowest level of the castle just after sunset. He turned, surprise, lust and confusion all slamming into his gut like a physical blow. "You come to me early tonight, my wolf. Am I to think you could not wait to see me or should I worry something has happened?"

"You already know I couldn't wait to see you." Reinn moved closer, his gaze traveling over Bronwen's body in such a seductive way that surely would have had all the blood pooling in his cock if he had the time to drink so soon after waking. "And nothing has happened yet but it will."

"Calliope?" Fear was a sharp dagger in his gut. He took a step toward Reinn, his hands fisted at his sides. "Is she alright?"

"We have to tell her everything tonight, Bronwen. The complete truth. No more holding back and no more secrets."

The seriousness in Reinn's tone had Bronwen lifting a brow to study his friend, his lover, his wolf. Reinn was often a moody sort, definitely one prone more to mischief and play, even anger rather than seriousness. It alarmed Bronwen to hear it now even as a light spark of anger flashed. Since when did his wolf make the decisions in this castle? Even as he wondered the question, he knew it was not the shift of control causing his unease but the simple emotion of pure dread. He had been putting off the truth, content to continue the façade especially now that the three of them had found a sort of happiness together. He wanted nothing to take away the contentment they built, the sheer gleam of joy that brightened their woman's face, the light she had brought into their own seemingly endless dark.

"Why the sudden rush?" Bronwen turned and moved to a table near the still fire place along the far wall. He poured a goblet of the blood-laced wine he kept on hand and drank half of it down in a single gulp. It trickled through him, offering only a minute respite to the building hunger that ate at him upon first waking. He would need more blood to rid himself of the animalistic need to feed, more to give his cold body the strength to assimilate life until the sun rose again. "I thought we were working our way to that point, taking it slow, preparing her to accept."

"She's planning a wedding celebration for the three of us and she wishes to have it here at the castle. No doubt she intends to invite all in the lands and you can be sure she will hold all of this in the sunlight."

Bronwen took another sip, this one slower, smaller, contemplative. He turned to Reinn, just as slowly, just as pensively. "She told you this?"

"Not all but most. She plans to tell you, too. Tonight, likely rather soon this night. I doubt she will waste any time. I thought I would get to you first, give you a warning of fun to come." He flashed a grin at that, but it was only a shadow of his usual mischief, more rueful instead.

"And you do not think we can stop her plans without revealing all?" Bronwen turned back to the table, set down the now empty goblet, and immediately wished he had decided to refill it.

"I don't think we should try. You said yourself we should stop with secrets. We cannot continue to go on this way. You know that as well as I. The new moon is in a week's time, Bronwen. One week for whatever is going to happen because of the spell over her to happen."

"The monsters, the darkness and death," Bronwen said grimly. "Has it not already happened? Are we not the monsters?"

Reinn stepped to him and brushed the backs of his fingers down his cheek in a surprisingly tender gesture for the wolf. "We are monsters and that tears you apart. I know it does, lover, but I don't think we are the monsters she has to worry about. I know we are not! Neither of us would ever harm her. But *they* would. They would and they will. If they get to her we have only one chance to save her."

"The monsters we are have only one chance." Bronwen understood and he knew Reinn was right. To protect Calliope, to save her, they would have to fight monster to monster. To do that without losing her in the end, she would have to know what he and Reinn truly were.

"You brought her here. Destiny may have set us up for the fall, but you chose to follow through."

Bronwen stiffened, his head jerking away from Reinn's touch as anger flared. He needed no reminder that she was here at his insistence. "You have not hesitated to reap the advantages of her presence, wolf."

"No, I have not." Reinn spoke coolly now with an underlining arrogance that fueled Bronwen's anger even as it aroused his cock. "I have seen my destiny in her as well and I can't help but thank her for finally giving me you." He caught Bronwen's chin in his hand and held his face still. "We are meant. We all know it. It's time for her to know exactly what she is meant for, what as well as who she shares her body, mind and soul."

Bronwen closed his eyes and nodded, knowing in this too Reinn was right. "I need to feed. When I return we will go to her and tell her together." He curled his fingers around Reinn's wrist, holding for the simple need to hold, his mind already fumbling with the words to explain the natures of their beasts to Calliope.

"Your supply is running low." Reinn's thumb grazed Bronwen's closed lips. "I haven't been able to find much for you lately."

"Because they are getting to them first?" He had already realized his supply of fresh animal blood was waning. Reinn hunted for him on most occasions, entertaining his wolf's need to run, to track while keeping Bronwen's cabinet of blood filled from that of the animals Reinn preyed upon. He had taken to drinking animal blood long ago, taught to do so by he who sired him instead of taking blood from the other beings who inhabited the lands. To prevent him from becoming the complete monster he could so easily be. After becoming all but trapped in the castle grounds, however, after they began to realize how he and Reinn lived, the pickings of fresh animals started to run slim.

"Feed from me tonight." When Bronwen started to shake his head, Reinn quickly objected, his fingers gripping harder to Bronwen's chin. "It will be faster and save some of what is left for another night."

"You will have to shift, wolf. To take from you all I will need to survive this night as you are will not satisfy the hunger anymore. It is animal blood I have come to crave."

"Then it is animal blood you'll have." Reinn released his chin and let his hand graze down Bronwen's neck, his throat, dipping inside the material of his shirt to toy with the silky patch of curls on his chest.

Bronwen needed no more blood in his veins than the little he consumed through the wine to feel the arousal from the touch, from the promise of pure ecstasy in Reinn's eyes. Already, the electric green was beginning to darken, to turn a yellowish-gold around the rim, the pupils turning to slits.

"A partial change should do well enough." His hands dropped to Reinn's pants where he skillfully began to undo their ties. "If I am to use you to feed my hunger, I wish to have both parts of you, man and wolf."

He heard the agreement of the wolf in the guttural rumble Reinn made as Bronwen pulled his cock free of his breeches. He was only slightly hard and Bronwen thrilled at the feel of the length of meat growing in his hand. He kept his gaze on Reinn, stroking his shaft and watching as his eyes completed the change. Still, in their dark green and yellow rimmed depths, he saw the knowledge and desires of the man.

Reinn's face changed, bones shifting, his complexion going a deep rich brown. His nose elongated. His lips and cheeks moved to form a snout. His ears remained much in the same but for the point that shaped the top. His hands and fingers altered and grew, impossibly long claws extending from his fingertips and velvety soft golden hair coated most of his arms, his neck, and his chest.

He did not speak. Bronwen knew it would sound of more animal than man if he did. Even with only a partial change, the beast controlled that much. Still, Bronwen needed no words. The look in Reinn's eyes was enough. With his hand curled tightly around Reinn's now impossibly wide and deliciously long cock, Bronwen sank to his knees. He tipped his head back and found the wolf gazing down at him, saw the ragged rise and fall of his shoulders and chest as excitement and anticipation settled.

It made him smile even as a pang of regret for all the lost years, all the wasted time shot through his blackened heart. What was that time when one had eternity? Everything, for even eternity ended at some point. He had learned that long ago.

Rein's hand dove into Bronwen's hair, the claws grazing his scalp but not breaking the skin. Bronwen felt the tug and knew it was both Reinn's way of encouraging him to do what they both wanted and telling him it was okay. Careful, he would have to be so careful to accomplish this act as close to the edge of his hunger as he was, so aroused by the wolf offering himself to him, by the man submitting in such a way he rarely did. Already, the sharp point of his fangs had pierced his gums. Bronwen angled his head, licking first the smooth, slightly paler flesh of Reinn's shaft, reveling in the salty-sweet taste of the pre-cum that dribbled down from the head, of the sweat coating his skin, of man and beast. He moaned, the sound wrenched from his throat in a pleasured moment of sheer erotic enjoyment.

His tongue traveled the length of Reinn's cock, stopping only to lap at more pre-cum flowing almost freely now from the slit on the engorged head before taking the rod of meat inch by inch into his mouth. Though he continued cautiously, he knew his fangs, now fully extended in the thrill of arousal and blood lust, scraped Reinn's shaft as Bronwen sucked his cock down. Reinn's claws fisted his hair, the sharpest of pricks stinging Bronwen's scalp as Reinn's careful control snapped a little more.

The scent of blood permeated the air. Not from the shallow abrasions to his head, Bronwen knew, but from that which pumped through Reinn's veins. He felt it move through the vein in the underside of Reinn's cock and suppressed a pleased smile when Reinn tensed as he caressed that purplish throb with his tongue. The reverberation of fear was subtle but palpable and extremely tasty. Bronwen rode on that gentle wave for a long moment, his tongue stroking and following that vein, his throat muscles contracting around the shaft as he swallowed it down and slowly drew away.

He reached between Reinn's legs and marveled at the way they trembled slightly as he found Reinn's balls and cupped them. Reinn was growling now, unintelligible sounds that could have been moans or even words of encouragement from a man's voice. Bronwen locked his lips around the base of Reinn's cock, painstakingly careful to keep his fangs as far from the flesh as he could manage as he eased back and allowed Reinn's dick to fall from his mouth.

It was the scent of blood that drew his attention once more. The sweet coppery treat teased his senses, tightened his balls, and tormented everything from his fangs, to his heart, to his cock. He turned his head slowly, moving that fraction of an inch to taste the warm flesh of Reinn's inner thigh where the blood flowed through the artery like a river of his favorite beverage.

Bronwen had a fleeting thought that he despised this part of himself, the monster that drove him to do what he was about to do. Then he felt Reinn's encouraging hand in his hair, heard the growl that sounded of both plea and pleasure and sank his fangs into that softest and most sensitive of flesh. The first gush was nothing short of pure ecstasy, the warm rush of blood into his mouth the greatest pleasure of his demon-wrought existence. Reinn would feel much in the same, he knew, for the beast inside him could share in the pleasure, dance with the erotic thrill of being pleasured and taken as offering. His hand closed once more around Reinn's cock, squeezed and stroked as he drank from the wolf's inner thigh. When he felt the meat in his hand stiffen and shutter, he eased back on his bite only enough to let the cum that flowed from Reinn's explosive release to slide down his body and into Bronwen's mouth. It mixed with the blood, created a concoction that was equal parts intoxicating and rich, and only then did Bronwen feel his hunger, his beast feed to its fullest.

It was the sound from the doorway that penetrated the sexual euphoria. A quiet gasp followed by the word, "No," spoken over and over, growing louder and louder like a mantra of immense terror. Bronwen yanked back, his attention whirling to the door, to where Calliope stood frozen in the opening. Her eyes were wide and horror filled, her flesh paler than his own and her lips continued to move in that single word. "No."

The world stopped. In that moment everything hung in the balance of a stilled universe of shock and fear. Bronwen knew what she saw, not just two men, not just her lovers enjoying an escapade of oral sex. Beasts, monsters, one half changed and sated with blood trickling down his inner thigh while the other knelt on his knees before the animal with sharp and deadly teeth protruding from a mouth coated in that blood and come. His muscles grew stiff, his mind unable to process the sheer revulsion she must be feeling. He wanted to say something, to go to her, to hold her, but before he could find an ounce of his abilities to do so, she gave one final screamed, "No," and bolted from the room.

"Go after her." Reinn roared the command, the man managing to say the words through the control of the beast that still possessed him. "She can't go outside."

Bronwen did not have to be told twice. Fear pushing him as much as his love for her, he lunged to his feet, embraced his powers of speed, and chased after Calliope.

* * * *

Calliope ran. Blinded by tears and fear, she knew not where she was headed or what she would do when she got there. She only knew she had to get away. Monsters. They were both monsters. The image of them flicked in her mind, the hair covering Reinn's face and body, his very misshapen face and body, the teeth and blood on Bronwen's mouth and the eyes, both sets of eyes filled with such predatory, animalistic hunger and horror.

She burst through the back door to the veranda and was nearly at the steps when Bronwen appeared in front of her, a streak of blurry white in the air the only warning of something there before she saw him. She stopped in her tracks, backed up several steps, her hands coming up to shield herself, her head shaking wildly.

"Do not touch me." She could not stop the tears as they flooded her eyes and streamed down her face. Her voice was shrill. She wanted to sound brave, needed to be but she found herself quivering instead, shrinking away. "Get away from me. Please, do not hurt me."

"I would never hurt you, little one." Bronwen's voice, the smooth and tender voice she had come to love. How could it come from the face of a monster now? "Let us go back inside. We will explain everything."

"No." She shook her head harder now, more defiant. She would not go back inside this place where two monsters lived waiting to do…what? By the guardians, what did they plan to do to her? "Move out of my way, B…B…" She could not say his name. This was not Bronwen, not her heart, her destined. "Beast!"

Courage growing within her from places she did not know existed, she launched herself forward and miraculously sprinted passed him before he could grab her. Her ankle twisted as it hit the ground off the veranda but she did not let it stop her.

"Calliope, wait! Do not go out there. It is not safe."

She did not listen but continued to run. Even when she caught the pale blur out of the corner of her eye, she ran. When Bronwen appeared before her again, she merely changed her direction to go around him. The next blur was not so pale, not so close. In barely a blink, it swept Bronwen out of sight. It was the third blur that took her down.

Calliope landed on the ground with such force that the breath left her lungs and her head thudded. For a moment, the saw only darkness but then, as her vision cleared once more she saw the horrors. Snarling faces, elongated claws and jagged teeth hovered over her. One razor sharp clawed hand caught the material of her gown and ripped it to tatters. She did not scream, could not with the fear lodged so completely in her throat. It was her nightmare, the monsters that haunted her dreams come to the reality of night, and she was dead.

No. Not dead, she realized with a chill that froze the blood in her veins. *One shall be engulfed by a world of darkness to reside in terror and face a monster that will bring a death of no end.* They would not kill her, at least, not exactly. They would make her one of them, a death to be transformed into a monster that would never die.

* * * *

Reinn pushed for the change, the shifting of the remaining bones in his body causing him to roar in agony. It was always worse when he initiated the change rather than allowing it to come over him as it would through hunger or arousal. When it was the beast's idea it was an easy, virtually painless transformation. When it was the man who wished it, it simply hurt like a demon!

With barely enough breath in his lungs to keep him upright, his muscles screaming from the torment, he bolted from the bedchamber a fully changed wolf with only one prey in mind. The bastards would not have her. They would not harm her. And they would not have Bronwen.

The score was just short of carnage when he barreled into the back grounds. He didn't need his heightened sight to spot Calliope surrounded by the wolves of the pack. They had ripped her dress and one was hovering over her, his lower body between her thighs but fully clothed. He hadn't forced himself inside her. Yet.

A cry of sheer agony drew his gaze and he saw Bronwen go down. It hadn't been his scream but one of the wolves he had gotten the best of. Still, there were more circling him, preparing to attack, more than he would ever be able to fight off alone. Only three held Calliope while double that were after Bronwen. Torn between the woman of his destiny and the man of his heart, Reinn chose.

He ran faster than the wind, building the strength he would need with each contact of paw to ground and pounced. He hit hard, instinct more than plan had him rolling the wolf off of Bronwen, pinning the beast beneath his sharpened claws. "Go." He growled and knew the word was barely discernable as anything more than a roughened sound. He focused harder on speaking as man, on forming the words. "Get her to the mountaintop. She will be safe there."

* * * *

The snarling snout closed in on her face and Calliope closed her eyes. No good to weep, she told herself, pointless to scream or fight. Later she might loath herself for not fighting any longer, for simply giving in. But this was fate after all, her destiny.

She felt the warmth of its breath on her face, smelled the stench, and then jolted when the weight atop her was suddenly gone and she was yanked off the ground as though she weighed little more than a feather. Wind blew passed her with such an amazing force she almost felt nothing at all. Strong arms enveloped her and held her tight against a hard body. Only when her feet touched pebbled ground did she finally open her eyes. She gasped as Bronwen sank to the ground in front of her, doubled over by the pain of his obvious wounds.

"Calliope! Thank the guardians, you are safe." Aithne rushed to her side, her hand immediately pawing over Calliope as she searched for injuries. "You are, are you not?"

"Aithne, how did you..."

"Little one, answer your sister. Are you hurt?" Bronwen's voice was tight, his face a careful mask as he stood.

Instinct had Calliope reaching for her sister, pushing her behind her. "I am not hurt," she said more to ease Aithne's mind than Bronwen's. He was covered in blood, his shirt torn to expose a deep gash at his abdomen. There were more cuts and scrapes on his face, his neck but even as she watched they began to heal.

"You..." She heard the word leave her mouth but did not know what she had been about to say.

"I have to go back. I have to help Reinn."

"You have to stay here." Aithne stepped around Calliope and might have walked to Bronwen, but Calliope caught her arm, stopping her. She covered Calliope's hand with her own and gave her a smile of both understanding and comfort. "You are safe here, both of you. Karan has gone for Reinn. She will bring him here as well."

"Karan! But the monsters, the beasts, and Reinn is..."

"We know." Aithne brought her free hand to Calliope's cheek. "Karan will be safe. She is the only one of us who can get Reinn out of there."

"She is the only one who did. Damn, what a battle."

Calliope whirled to find Karan behind her, struggling unsuccessfully not to drop a barely conscious Reinn on the rocky mountaintop. He had transformed, gone was the half-man and half-beast she had seen in the bedchamber with Bronwen. He looked instead as he had the moment she first saw him in the foyer of the castle save for the blood and the deep gashes to his neck, his chest, his stomach, and legs.

"Is he," Calliope gulped as tears blurred her vision, "dead?" The last came on a barely audible whisper as she took a tentative step toward him. Her heart forgot the beast of the stilled man who lay but a few feet away, remembering only his mischievous grins and playful moods, his heated touches and fevered kisses.

"He's not dead." Karan's hand was beneath Reinn's head and she gently lowered it, allowing his head to rest on the ground. "But he's hurt badly."

"Move aside, little sister," Aithne said softly. "I can help him. I can heal him."

"But your powers are only to heal yourself." Was that not the gift Aithne had been given when she broke her part of the curse? The powers to heal from within. How could such a power be useful in helping another?

"I can heal him," Aithne said again, more insistently, more determinedly. "Trust me. I cannot explain how I know and I will not waste time trying. Trust me to do what I know." She hurried to Reinn's side, sank to her knees, and bowed her head, her hands moving over his wounds, not quite touching the mangled flesh.

Karan walked to Calliope and it was only when her sister's gaze flicked to her left that Calliope realized Bronwen now stood beside her.

"You're hurt, too." Karan looked at Bronwen, her gaze obviously searching.

"Not as badly as Reinn. I will heal my wounds. They are not as deep, as fatal."

"Then you can die. Both of you can die." Calliope whirled on him, a new and unexpected fear icing in her veins. From the moment she opened the door to the bedchamber and saw the men she loved for the monsters they truly are, she had thought only of getting away. Was it not because of her, of that rash action that they stood here now, that Reinn lay fighting for his life, monster or man, now?

"Yes, little one. We can both die." Bronwen's eyes sparkled with what Calliope was certain were tears as he glanced at Reinn. Then he looked back at her, his lips thin, his jaw set. "Would you like to finish the job before I heal completely? I can tell you how to render certain death to a vampire such as me. Perhaps Karan could as well."

A vampire. A monster. A blood drinking demon of the dark. Calliope had heard tales of such creatures, of the horrors they inflicted, the lives they claimed. But just now, she saw only her Bronwen, her destined, her love. Vampire or not, he was no monster. She could see that now, feel it in everything she knew, everything she was.

Rather than answer his question, she asked one of her own. "Does Reinn possess the same powers? Can he heal himself as you can?" Reinn was not a vampire. That much was almost stupidly obvious.

She had also heard tales of others. Half-man and half-animal, it was not so uncommon in her world. There were after all centaurs and many other half-breeds. Those beings did not transform though, they did not maim and hunt as Reinn did, as a werewolf did.

"He does, but he is not strong enough to heal those wounds alone. They are too deep, too vicious, too many." Bronwen's voice broke on the last. He shook his head and let his gaze drop to the ground.

"But with Aithne's help, he will heal." Karan reached out and touched Bronwen's shoulder, her voice certain and calm.

With hardly a thought, Calliope reached too and clasped Bronwen's hand in hers. She knew he glanced at their joined hands, felt his light squeezed to hers, knew he looked at her then, but her gaze went to Karan. "How did you know?"

"Eric had a vision." Karan shrugged as if her explanation was absolutely normal. To her it likely was. Eric, her mate, possessed the power of sight. Calliope knew Eric often needed a tool such as a crystal or bowl of water to see a vision, but sometimes they came to him without aide and completely unbidden.

"Is he here with you?" She had not seen anyone but her two sisters. Still, much of her focus before now had been on Bronwen and Reinn.

"He's in Tolynn. I poofed us both there, left him with Hakan and Dustin, snatched Aithne and brought us here. I can only transport two at a time and when it comes time to return I'll have my hands full with all of you. Besides, this was for the women to do, the sisters, the three hearts."

"I can help." Bronwen's voice sounded tight and Calliope saw him wince. The gash to his chest and abdomen were taking the longest to heal. "I cannot poof, as you say, but I can move faster than the eye can see."

"It will likely come in handy, too." Karan reached into the pocket of the long overcoat she wore and pulled out some sort of sealed cup. She held it out for Bronwen and tipped her head back as if scanning the sky. "Time may turn into a factor if we have to stay here too long. Drink this. It will help."

Bronwen took the cup without question. "As long as there is time for the initial trip, it will not be a factor." Their gazes met and something passed between them, a kind of knowledge that Calliope could not read. Bronwen opened the cup, drank deep, and made a face so repulsive it was nearly comical. "What is this or dare I ask?"

Karan's lips kicked into a grin. "Blood. Animal blood. It is what you prefer, isn't it? I don't know what kind of animal. Hakan shoved it in my hand before we left Tolynn." She cocked her head and ginned even wider. "I take it not all taste the same."

"No." Though he did not make the sound, there was a distinctive yuck lining the word.

"But any blood will help to enhance your healing, will it not?" Aithne asked, moving to stand by Karan.

"It will. What about Reinn? Did your powers help enhance his as well?"

"He will be okay. He is healing and much quicker now, but he will need time yet before he will be fully healed."

"Then we wait," Bronwen said and gave Calliope's hand another squeeze, though his gaze like hers remained transfixed on Reinn.

"And hope we don't run out of time," Karan muttered. "This ground is safe but only until light. They will find it by sunrise. Of course, by that time no ground will be safe for you unless you intend to go beneath it."

"The sun, you cannot go in the sun." Calliope reflexively jerked at Bronwen's hand as the tales she had heard came back to her in vivid detail. "That is why you were never there with me, with us, in the day. We have to find you somewhere else to go before sunrise. Karan, you can do it, poof him somewhere."

"Sister, I can't leave you, Aithne and Reinn. Bronwen and I are the only two who can get us off this mountaintop fast enough. The instant we leave this protected ground they will be on us."

"Who are they?" Calliope demanded, nearly screaming in her frustration and fear. "We keep saying they but who are they really? Monsters, werewolves like Reinn, but mean ones? Why are they out to kill us?"

Chapter Ten

Bronwen pulled his hand free and took a step back. He could not touch her now, needed distance if only a foot or two to collect his thoughts and finally, finally tell her the truth of everything. It was harder than it should have been, harder especially with Reinn still unconscious on the ground. She already knew most of it, the worst of it. That they were the monsters, in part or maybe even just as much as those who hunted them.

"They are the pack who made him, who turned Reinn into what he is now so long ago." His mind went back to that night, that time. He saw it all so clearly as if he were truly there again in the flesh. "We were attacked, Reinn by the leader of the werewolf pack, me by the lesser wolves who obeyed him. Before that, we were mortal, we were friends."

He stepped back and slowly lowered to rest on a huge rock. Calliope was watching him intently thinking…what? She did not look so horrified anymore and yet she did. Not horrified by him, he realized, not so repulsed now by him and Reinn but by the story he was telling, the terrible outcome she would know was coming.

"We came to this world on a vacation of sorts and ended up in the wrong place at the wrong time, as the saying goes. It was dark, the moon full and large, and we were attacked." He closed his eyes, but the memories of that night, of the battle between mortals and monsters was too vivid in the dark behind his lids. Opening his eyes again, he went on. "They went after Reinn first. By *they* I mean the leader of the pack and another of his wolves. I tried to get to him, to help him, but the others were on me too fast. They held me down, took blood from me, ate at my flesh." He saw Calliope's face pale so much it nearly glowed white in the darkness of the night and bile rose in his throat. He had not meant to be so grotesque, but she had to know the whole of it now and that meant every gory detail as well.

"Why are you not a werewolf?" Karan crossed her arms under her breasts, her brows raised in question. "If you were attacked by werewolves, it stands to reason you would be a werewolf too, not a vampire."

"There was a vampire among those who attacked me."

"He was their protector," Karan said almost in a whisper as understanding crossed her face.

"You understand more of this dark world than I thought."

"Vampires, werewolves, beasts of the night, it is a huge money maker in the mortal realm. Still, they have most of their facts right it seems. Vampires are stronger than werewolves, able to kill faster and withstand more."

"We are."

"So it was the vampire who feasted on you and not the werewolves."

"Feasted." Bronwen laughed scornfully. "That would be a perfect term for it. The werewolves ate at me, tore at my flesh, but it was the vampire who drained me of my mortal life. He did not change me but left me for dead."

"And Reinn? What happened to Reinn? And how are you here?" Calliope's voice was small, quiet, the words of her questions trembling as her breaths came in ragged bursts.

Bronwen forced himself to meet her sad, appalled gaze. He hated to put that look on her face, to see such detest and grief in her lovely eyes. "Reinn was changed. The leader made it his business to take Reinn himself. As for me, another vampire came to my rescue, our rescue I should say. He fought off the werewolves. So many of them." He shook his head, still disbelieving how many werewolves Delamort had taken on single-handedly in addition to the other vampire. "He killed a few. I do not know for certain exactly how many he managed to kill before he jerked me and Reinn up and fled with us to the castle. It angered them, of course, so much so that they have been out for revenge since. They wish to kill me as they failed to do that night and to take Reinn into their pack as he was meant to be from the start."

"He saved you. The other vampire took your life and this one gave you another." Calliope moved slowly to his side, her steps hesitant as if she feared he might push her away. When he simply watched her progress, saying nothing, she tentatively lowered to her knees between his legs. Her hands framed his face, shaking hands so cold to the touch he recognized their chill even with the constant cold of his own flesh. "I owe him much, this other vampire who saved you."

Tears welled. Bronwen stared at her through the shimmering discolored mist in his eyes and felt a relief so overpowering it rendered him speechless for a long moment. When at last he found the words, he covered her hands with his own and held them tight. "Calliope, my dear sweet little one." He turned his face into one of her hands and brushed his lips to her palm. "I too owe him everything."

"All this time, you and Reinn have lived in that castle, what, hiding out from the pack of werewolves and the mean vampire?" Aithne spoke for the first time since he began his story. She had taken a seat on the ground where she had stood and pulled her legs to her chest, hugging them close to her rounded belly. "What happened to the one who saved you? What was his name?"

"Delamort. He died some time later. He..." Bronwen broke off, the words catching somewhere in his throat. "He wanted to see the sunlight."

"He walked out in the day on purpose?" Karan gasped. "That's suicide."

"It is, yes. He stayed with Reinn and I, raised us to understand how to cope with the monsters we had become, taught me to use the powers I had been given when I became vampire, the powers used to keep the castle protected from the outside. I was to protect Reinn, you see, always to be there to keep him safe." He looked to Reinn now, his friend still lying motionless on the ground several paces away. "I failed."

"You did not fail." Calliope's hands jerked on his face and turned him back to look at her. "You did all you could to protect both of us. If anyone is to blame for what happened this night, it is I."

"You did not know. I did not tell you. I was afraid...I love you so much, Calliope."

"And I love you." She glanced at Reinn's still form. "Both of you. So much so that I cannot say tonight would have turned out any differently had you told me rather than me walking in on you. It was such a shock, to learn the men I love are the monsters I thought to fear. But it is not you or Reinn I have to fear. It was them, the pack, and we are away from them now. We are safe and both of you, all of us, are okay."

"Anyone else getting the sense we aren't the only ones hanging around out here anymore?"

Karan's whisper had Bronwen holding tighter to Calliope's hands, pulling them down as he slowly looked around. He could see them, the greenish-golden eyes of the approaching werewolves, the others who hid among the foliage and trees.

"We are not alone anymore." Bronwen spoke quietly, his mind already reeling as he fought to come up with a plan for escape. Damnit, he was the only man capable of protecting these women and yet he knew not how to get them each off this mountaintop alive.

"It's time to move then." Karan shot a glance at the sky then penned Bronwen with a steady glare. "You know we are but hours from sunrise."

"Yes. We should not need hours to figure out how to get you out of here safely."

"No. We shouldn't and we won't. I already know how it can be done. The problem is where we are going it will already be nearing light. The sun rises sooner there. You will have but minutes, not hours when you reach the goddess queen's land."

"We are going home?" Calliope stood, her face a mixture of excitement, confusion, and disbelief.

"It is the only place where Bronwen and Reinn will be safe from these monsters. Mother has no rule over these dark lands, but she has already set up protections in our palace. Once you are safely there, she will use her powers to ensure you will be forever safe from these monsters and all others."

"But first, we have to get you there," Aithne chimed in.

"I can take only one with me and I will not have the strength to return for another until it is too late," Karan explained. "That leaves you," she held Bronwen's gaze, "to take the other two. Reinn is healing quickly but he is still too weak to be of any use to us. I think I should take him and you take Calliope and Aithne."

Bronwen was already shaking his head. No way. No fucking way. "You should take your sisters. I will bring Reinn."

"You're not listening. Pig headed males. You're as bad as Eric and the rest of them, always looking to protect the woman." Karan's muttering had him wanting to chuckle even in the direness of the situation. "I can only take one with me. That one needs to be the one who cannot fight for himself. That one will be Reinn. You're fast enough to get the three of you out of here and to safety without the werewolves catching you. And, if by some terrible chance something happens, Calliope and Aithne are not too helpless to fight back. Hell, they can run and hide if nothing else!"

"Thanks," Aithne grumbled and shot her sister a scornful look.

"Don't mention it." Karan beamed a quick smile that faded just as briskly. "You know the way to the palace of the goddess queen, I presume."

Of course he did. She knew he did. It was merely her way of telling him there would be no more arguing. He saw in that moment where Calliope got her strength beneath the timorous demeanor she often showed when first coming into his life. "Your sister is a brave one," he told Calliope as he stood, "as you have become as well. Promise me you will not become as hardheaded as she is too."

Calliope gave a watery, nervous laugh. "I will promise nothing of the sort."

Bronwen forced a smile and drew her into his arms. "Yes, I feared that would be your answer. Shall we do this?" He looked down at her first and then held out an arm for Aithne.

Karan was already making her way to Reinn, lifting him with only the slightest show of effort to his feet, supporting his substantial weight with her shoulder under one of his arms. "As we say in my world, on three."

"On three," Bronwen agreed. For the first time in more millenniums than he could count, he said a silent prayer and embraced his powers as tightly as he held the women in his arms.

* * * *

Calliope recognized the spot. It was Aithne's favorite place in the land of the goddess queen; a secluded path near the back of the grounds in the wood leading to a cove of jagged rocks and thick brush. A thin stream ran through those rocks, trickling down with a quiet and peaceful, almost musical sound. And high in the sky to the east the enormous ball of sunlight was just beginning to peak in the horizon.

"Bronwen!" Fear slammed into her hot and fast. His arm around her loosened and he fell to one knee, his head bowed. "Aithne, help me! The sun, we must get him out of the sun." Panicked, she tried to pull him to his feet but ended up on her knees in front of him when he resisted. His hand came up, blindly finding her face to cup her cheek.

"It is too late, little one." He spoke softly, his voice weak, as was his touch.

"No. No. It cannot be too late." She would not believe that, could not. "The sun is barely out. If we hurry…"

"If it were going to kill him he would be dust by now." Aithne's gentle hands on her shoulders had Calliope tipping her head back to look up at her sister. "Bronwen? What is happening?"

"I...I do not know." Slowly, he lifted his head. Calliope knew it was not her or Aithne he looked at but the sun. He blinked, made an "Ah," sound of pain, then blinked again before squinting at the rising ball of blinding light.

"Bronwen?" Calliope heard herself whisper, felt her hand move to cover his on her cheek, but it was all unconscious reactions. Her attention was on his face, on the pain she saw moving through his expression, of the fear that consumed his eyes. It was not a pain of agony, she realized as she watched him, but one of a man being given a gift he knew not how to accept. The fear was not a fear of what was being given but one that the gift would soon be wrenched from his grasp.

"There are stories in the mortal world of day walkers," Karan's told them as she approached from behind, "vampires that can walk in the light."

Calliope shot a disbelieving glance at her sister, looked back at Bronwen, and slowly pulled his hand from her face. "Could this be true? Could you be a day walker now?"

His gaze met hers and hope filled his eyes, glistened through the tears that welled in their depths. "If it is, then you have given me such a gift no other could possibly give."

"I gave you? But how? I had nothing do to with this." But even as she argued, she felt the truth settle in her belly, in her mind, in her heart. Power, so acutely obvious it could be nothing else. The power of light, of love, of destiny.

"Didn't you, lover?" Reinn's question had her leaping up and spinning around.

She gasped at the sight of him, standing straight and tall as he strode toward her with his masculine pride and mischievous grin tilting his so kissable lips. And in the electric green of his eyes she saw more power still, felt it swirl with that already noted inside her. This too of love, of destiny, but also of a controlled detachment.

"You are healed." She beamed a smile at him and extended her free hand. He took it in his, kissing the top of her hand in a stately gesture more common to Bronwen than Reinn.

"I am healed in more ways than simple wounds, my lady."

"The beast?" Bronwen stood and reached for Reinn, his fingers dancing along the side of Reinn's neck as his hand moved to cup Reinn's nape.

"Is still inside me but buried deeper than ever before. There is no constant desire to change, no fight within me to hold him back, to keep the wolf at bay."

Calliope's gaze danced between the two men, her men, her lovers, both truly alive with unmarred flesh as if the battle with the werewolves never happened. But it *had* happened and it had changed all three of them in ways they were just discovering and possibly other ways they did not yet know.

"How can you believe I had anything to do with this?" She focused on Reinn, searching his eyes for the knowledge he so obviously held as truth. She could not grasp it. Then she looked at Bronwen with the same wonderment. "How can either of you think this?"

"Because you had everything to do with it, daughter."

Calliope's eyes grew wide even as love swam into her heart. She turned, her hands still locked with Bronwen's, with Reinn's so that her arms ended up crossed at her waist, and found not only the goddess queen approaching but the king, Dustin, Hakan, Eric and... She blinked, her jaw falling open in shock. For a moment she was certain her vision played a trick on her.

"Daria." Aithne confirmed Calliope's surprise with a quiet gasp of her own.

"Well, if it isn't the wicked goddess of our worlds," Karan muttered under her breath.

Daria's stunning lips quirked ever so slightly and Calliope feared for an instant she might have heard Karan. She was lovely and decidedly wicked in her glory. Her mane of hair matched that of Ina's and Calliope's in the golden sunshine shade bright enough to blind. Her skin gleamed with as much smooth and flawlessness as radiating power. She wore a gown of lilac so fitting and stunning Calliope would not have been surprised to see the men around them standing with their jaws hanging open.

"Your mother is right, though it was not only you but all of you who formulated the events of the past night, of the previous phases of our moons. You have done well." She stepped away from Ina, Andrew and the men and sashayed, Calliope could think of no other word for the way Daria moved, to Aithne. "I must admit I am surprised." She smiled conspiratorially and leaned her cheek to Aithne's, her gaze pointedly on Dustin and Hakan. "I bet it was not an easy task giving up one for the other."

"I still have them both in my life." Aithne's words were tight even with the confusion and suspicion that coated her voice. "That is what matters most."

"So I guess it is. So I guess it is," Daria repeated and stepped to Karan. "And you, the middle daughter, the odd one of the three, the one who never quite fit in."

"I have found my place," Karan said dryly.

Daria threw back her head and laughed, a truly musical sound that had birds in the distance joining in the song. "Indeed you have. But yours was not an easy search. Not so easy to give yourself to a man or to his world."

"It was worth it in the end." Karan looked to Eric and only then did her expression soften, a hint of a smile coming to her lips.

"So it was," Daria agreed. "Then there is you, Calliope." She moved once more to stand beside Calliope but Bronwen and Reinn flanked her, not allowing Daria to get any closer, keeping her out of their circle. "The prettiest, the fairest, the one with the worst fate, you gave yourself to not one but two monsters willingly."

Calliope tightened her hold on both men. "Neither are true monsters."

"Yes, you have come to believe that now, to love both despite the truth you know. It is because of this that they now share in this new power."

"This new power?" Calliope repeated, swamped with an icy chill of uncertainty. She knew something had changed, felt it in her very being, but it was not a sense of power, not what she expected to feel as such.

"As long as they are with you the vampire will walk by day and the werewolf will remain at bay." Daria paused as if to allow her words to sink in. "You see, Calliope, even a goddess has her limitations. I cannot turn your vampire mortal once more nor can I take away the beast inside your wolf, but I can make their existences easier, happier, and, shall we say, more manageable."

"It was all a test." Karan's statement drew everyone's attention. She looked, Calliope thought and had to bite the inside of her lip to keep from grinning, like a very irate, very sexy wood nymph. "The curse, the certain death, fate, destined hearts, it was all a freaking test!"

"Yes and no," Daria answered vaguely. "The spell was real. This, I promise you. I did cast the spell over each of you. One of you will suffer at the hands of desire so greatly it will bring you death from the inside out. Another shall suffer a heart so divided that fear shall bring her death. Lastly, one shall be engulfed by a world of darkness to reside in terror and face a monster that will bring a death of no end. Had either of you made different choices, had either of you been weaker of will, of mind, of heart, the outcome of all would have been far different."

"Each part, each choice led to the final end, to here," Calliope whispered as understanding dawned. Of course, thinking back, she could see now how it all related. "Aithne had to choose between Hakan and Dustin. Her choice broke her part of the spell."

"And empowered her with the ability to heal." Daria nodded.

"An ability she used on both herself and, in the end, on Reinn tonight to save him." Calliope looked from Aithne to Reinn and saw in their expressions as they understood as well. "Karan gained the ability to move between the worlds," she went on after a moment, not really talking to those around her as much as simply thinking out loud, piecing together all the steps to what was turning out to be a pretty amazing puzzle. "Combine that with Eric's visions and she knew what was happening at the castle tonight, used her powers to come to this world, grab Aithne, and save Reinn from the werewolves."

Reinn winced. "I'm starting to feel like a real pussy here, always the one being rescued, first from the big bad wolves and then from sudden death. It's humiliating!"

Karan chuckled. "Lucky for you we intend to stay close by from now on."

"Yeah, lucky for me." Reinn rolled his eyes and Calliope had to smile.

"Do not be such a baby."

"You have summed up the past weeks nicely, daughter." Ina walked to Calliope, stepping behind her, and hugging her close. "You also understood far quicker than I or your father."

"Then you did not know all of this was a test?" Calliope looked back over her shoulder at her mother's lovely face, praying she had not known, had not led her and her sisters to believe the threat to be far greater than it was.

"Of course not! I have been as frightened your whole lives as you have been since I first revealed the spell to you the night of Aithne's celebration."

"The threat was real," Daria told her as if reading her thoughts. With the little Calliope truly knew of the goddess it was possible she had read her mind. "As I said, had either of you made different choices, the outcome would have been far different. Aithne could have been killed by the poison she ingested had she not found the faith in herself to choose between her men. Karan could have been killed by the men who kidnapped her had she not found her faith to believe in her man."

"And I could have died tonight if I had not found my faith to believe in the love I already felt for my men."

"Precisely." Daria nodded in a stiff approval.

"Yet, with all you have pieced together, you still do not see your power in all of this." King Andrew did not move from his place but the deep timbre of his voice drew everyone's attention.

Calliope shook her head. "I gained no real power as Aithne and Karan did aside from what you said of Bronwen now walking in the light and Reinn keeping the wolf at bay." She glanced at Daria. "But those are not powers of my own as you said you changed that for them."

"The power you hold is one you have possessed always. The only one of my daughters to hold a true power." Ina hugged her closer and brushed a sweet kiss to her cheek. "Love, my darling Calliope. You have said yourself on many occasions that there can be no greater power than love. It is but the one gift that can shine through any dark and because of that power within you, you saw through it all to grasp your destiny with both your true hearts."

* * * *

"Even after all that has happened, I find myself agreeing with your sister." Reinn puffed out a breath as he bounced onto the bed in Calliope's bedchamber. He lay on his back, hands behind his head, feet crossed at the ankles and stared as the ceiling. "Daria really is the wicked goddess of the world."

Calliope turned and simply looked at him, her heart swirling with more emotions than she could count but two were paramount, love and thankfulness. She had nearly lost him, came so very close to never again having this man that she loved. "As with all things and beings, there is a good side as well as the bad, even in a goddess."

"It reminds me of a mortal tale." Bronwen sat on the edge of the bed and started to remove his boots. "The grandmother, or so she would be titled, cursing her grandchildren for power and stature." He shook his head and scowled. "And they consider my kind the demons."

"Daria cares of nothing more than our bloodline, the building of power, and the rule of the worlds." Calliope sat on her knees on the side of the bed and faced both her men. "It has always been that way. Mother defied law so long ago when she joined with my father for love rather than the one Daria had picked for her. In Daria's mind, our bloodline was tainted from that moment forward. My sisters and I are not goddesses as Daria and even Ina but we are demigoddesses, our powers diluted by the half-blood of our father."

"Powers you might have had sooner if not for the curse," Reinn pointed out, still staring at the ceiling.

Calliope had wondered about that, wondered if like her own power of love, Karan and Aithne had always possessed their powers as well. Only none of them had realized because the terms of the curse had dampened them in some way. "Perhaps." She slowly nodded. "But in Daria's mind, my sister's and I had to prove ourselves worthy to rule. We had to prove ourselves smart enough to make decisions with and without the involvement of our heart, brave enough to give and take, and, believe it or not, to love enough no matter the faults or circumstance."

"All of which the three of you did." Bronwen stood, unfastened his breeches and shucked them down his legs, then sat back down.

Calliope watched him with unabashed interest now. It was hard not too after all when one of her lovers was steadily getting naked before her eyes. Her nipples beaded and her pussy grew wet in response. For a long moment, her thoughts splintered, the shards she could catch pertaining only to the smooth, pale body bearing itself just out of her reach, and the feel of that flesh against her, *inside* her.

"All of which the three of us did," she finally managed to repeat even if the words sounded a bit breathless, decidedly hot.

"So, who will rule when the goddess queen Ina steps down?"

Reinn's nonchalant question told Calliope two things. First, he had not yet noticed Bronwen undressing and he could not care less who took the throne of the goddess queen when her mother's reign came to an end. Reluctantly, she tore her gaze from Bronwen and sighed.

"It appears as though it will be me, us, the three of us." Her stomach gave a tickling little flutter at the thought. As the youngest of three daughters, she had never really thought to rule someday. Tonight, however, she had come to realize it would be her place after all.

Both men looked at her, Reinn with one sexy brow raised and an expression of utter intrigue and Bronwen with a thin lipped expression of concern and expectance. It was Bronwen who spoke. "How do you feel about that, about our arrangement in the ruling court of this world? How do you think your people will feel?"

She had not yet had the chance to wonder about these questions, but did so now. How did she feel about someday being goddess queen? Excited, she supposed, nervous and important. As for her arrangement with Bronwen and Reinn that would mean for the first time in world history there would be two reigning kings rather than one. How would her people feel about that? She had no clue.

"I am uncertain of yet," she answered Bronwen honestly. "I shall let you know when I figure it out."

"But you're certain you will rule and not one of your sisters." Reinn pushed himself up on his elbows and studied Calliope.

"Aithne has her own land and, through she will likely never be queen of Tolynn, she and Dustin have no plans to ever leave that land or his command as the captain of the Tolynn guard. Karan is of another world now, Eric's world where she is the happiest she has ever been. She and Eric have a life, a business there. I am all that is left."

"You are the one that cares about this palace, the surrounding lands and people most," Bronwen interjected.

Calliope nodded. "That is true." She took a deep breath, pushed it out through pursed lips and then looked from Bronwen to Reinn and back again. "And at this moment the people of this land I want most are here in this room." She saw when understanding dawned in the bottomless dark of Bronwen's eyes. The corner of his mouth twitched just before he slowly dragged his tongue over his bottom lip and her stomach did a lovely and enthusiastic flop.

* * * *

Reinn saw the silent exchange pass between Calliope and Bronwen and felt more alive than he could ever remember. Perhaps surviving such a close brush with death for the second time in his life did that to a man. Certainly it left him changed, first by becoming a werewolf to hide in the dark, and now by the burial of that wolf so the man could be with the man and woman he loved.

The heat he saw moving between his lovers just now had his brows rising along with his cock. "You two want to share this little secret you've got going on?"

"Actually lover, I am sure you would agree it is a rather large secret." Bronwen removed his shirt and then turned on the foot of the bed, the move graceful and sexy as hell. He stopped on his hands and knees, the long curtain of his ebony hair obscuring one side of his handsome face, his hardened cock and balls dangling between his legs. Oh yeah, rather large indeed.

Calliope snickered and got to her feet to begin removing her gown. "And what we would prefer to share is you."

Reinn's pulse tripped even as arousal spiked. His balls gave a decided jump of anticipation inside his breeches as Bronwen crawled to him. The vampire straddled Reinn's legs and started to tug at his breeches. Reinn lifted his hips, aiding Bronwen as the man peeled the leather down Reinn's body. Bronwen leaned forward to kiss the flesh he exposed bit by tantalizing bit, taking care to detour around Reinn's already throbbing cock, his nose grazing lightly against the shaft and adding to the torturous need building in Reinn's balls.

Reinn sucked in a breath as Bronwen's teeth skimmed his inner thigh, his eyes closing on a strangled plea but not before he saw Calliope join them. She moved onto the bed beside him. Naked now, her body radiated a teasing heat that mixed with his arousal and put his senses on an even more heightened alert. He felt her hands join Bronwen's briefly as his breeches were removed and swept away. Then she was moving over him, her lithe body sliding across his to straddle his waist, the heat of her pussy a flame to the head of his screaming cock.

He opened his eyes to find her smiling down at him. Her hands were on either side of his head, her legs on either side of his hips, her pussy perfectly in position to ride him to sexual oblivion. He reached for her, his hands gripping her slender waist, but she resisted the tug down, battling his attempt to impale her by sheer will alone.

"It will not be fast this time, lover," she told him in a sultry voice that wafted over his flesh, flowing down his body to curl teasingly around his balls.

"You are ours this time." Bronwen's hands skimmed the inner side of Reinn's outstretched legs. "Ours to take. Ours to enjoy."

Gaze locked with his, Calliope gave him no time to respond before slowly lowering her body to his. Her pussy sheathed his cock inch by painstakingly torturous inch. Every attempt he made to thrust harder, to push deeper was met with a sure fire resistance he couldn't combat. It was agony of the most exquisite kind and he felt his mind go crazy with it, wanting to reject the torture even as it begged for more.

Calliope stopped when she had his cock buried inside her to the hilt and he couldn't stop the low guttural growl of protest. There was no animalistic rage in the sound, but the utter hunger of a man. It made her smile and he had to smile with her.

"Are you trying to kill me?" He gripped her hips harder, tried to move and groaned again when, rather than pulling back so he could plunge inside her, she rocked her body instead. Her pussy gyrated against his body. His cock so deeply lodged inside the fiery heat of her channel ached from the pleasure.

"No." Something moved through her expression, a kind of sadness he immediately wanted to make go away. "That has already come too close to happening this last day."

"But we are trying to drive you as wild as you do us." Bronwen's voice from down at Reinn's feet sounded just a bit arrogant and humorous.

"Think of it as the final taste of your destiny, Reinn." Calliope began to move, easing her body up, lowering it once more. His cock crept out, gradually entered again. "This is how it will be always for us." She did another gradual retreat, but when she lowered her body this time, she pounded down so abruptly Reinn sucked a startled breath through his teeth.

"Damn!" He ground the word as his eyes rolled back in his head. The pleasure of that single thrust ricocheted through his shaft and balls, splintering off to reach both his toes and his head with equal erotic delight.

Calliope laughed, the sound wickedly sensual. She laid her body on top of his, leaned in to capture his mouth in a feverish kiss, and rolled them until he was on top. Her legs spread wider as her hips came off the bed, pistoning her pussy onto his cock before he even had the wherewithal to take control. He found it quickly though, rearing back with his hips only to ruthlessly drive his cock completely inside her in such vicious thrusts she actually bit his tongue inside her mouth.

It was Bronwen's hands on Reinn's ass that stopped his thrusts, the chill of the other man's flesh a stilling shock to his overheated buttocks.

"Slow, lover." The humor remained in Bronwen's voice along with a deep arousal that promised much more than a tender graze of hand to bare butt cheeks. "I have discovered Calliope enjoys our controlling nature and wonderfully brisk fucking. As do I, of course. But I wonder..." The bed shifted as Bronwen positioned his body behind Reinn's, folding himself over Reinn's back. "If you can keep up such a fabulous pace inside our woman while I am inside you."

The thrill of that statement left Reinn speechless. He let his kiss with Calliope linger for another moment, her tongue sliding over his where she had bit him as if in silent apology, and Reinn drew away. Bronwen's hands moved to his hips and the other man lifted him even as Bronwen's cock entered his anus.

Reinn's eyes closed on the first wave of erotic sensation as Bronwen inched the wide head of his cock past the tight rim of muscle in Reinn's anus and then continued on. With only Bronwen's pre-cum for lubrication and absolutely no foreplay, the intrusion burned as much as it pleasured, the intense stretching of his anus magnifying the rapture in his own cock still lodged deep within Calliope's sweetly tight pussy. He wanted to push back, to take Bronwen's length all the way inside in a single mind-numbing thrust.

Reading him correctly, knowing exactly what he would want, Bronwen gave it to him. With a tight grip to his hips, Bronwen slammed the last three inches of his dick into Reinn's anus, the resulting insurmountable climb to sheer pleasure making Reinn grunt so loud he hardly heard Bronwen's echoing grunt or Calliope's cry as the brisk move rammed Reinn's cock more deeply inside her.

* * * *

It was amazing to watch when she could manage to keep her eyes open through the sensual waves of pulsing ecstasy soaring through her. The expressions on her men's faces as they joined together, as they joined with her, were one she would remember always. Her gaze met with Bronwen's over Reinn's shoulder and she caught the slight quiver of a smile through the hard concentration of his face. Though she knew not the sensations he felt at that moment, she had an idea what Reinn was experiencing. Bronwen had fucked her ass this way, and the mere memory had her pussy creaming around Reinn's cock, her anus puckering in remembered bliss.

"Ah, Gods!" Reinn ground the words through clenched teeth. Calliope laced her arms around his neck and felt his body tremble from his efforts to keep from crushing her from his and Bronwen's combined weight.

"You are not moving, lover," Bronwen taunted him, nipping at Reinn's ear, fucking his ass in the slowest of paces, driving Reinn's cock inside her channel in the sweetest and deepest of ways. "Does this mean you cannot handle a normal frantic pace after all?"

"Damn you, Bronwen," Reinn growled and moved. "Damn you, it feels too good. Both of you feel so fucking good!" He picked up pace with each word, managing somehow to move between Calliope and Bronwen until all three bodies were slapping together. Bronwen's dick in Reinn's ass, Reinn's cock ramming into her, it all became lost somewhere in a white-hot rush of crazed satisfaction. It was wild, frantic, and so very vicious it bordered the fine line between pleasure and pain.

Calliope loved it. The feel, watching them, being fucked by them, it was all too exquisite for words. She lost it. The orgasm swept over her, spewed out of her in an unwarranted and unexpected rush and she was powerless to stop it. Somewhere in the convulsion of her body, in the pulse hammering in her ears, she heard both men grunt on their own releases.

Sated and spent, Bronwen and Reinn collapsed on either side of her. Hearts pounding and breaths ragged, a contented sexual silence fell over the room. It was Reinn who spoke first, his hand moving lightly over Calliope's tummy in an idle caress.

"I love you, both of you. It is a power of the greatest kind that can shine through any dark."

"So I have often said." Calliope smiled, her hands absently caressing Reinn's shoulder and Bronwen's thigh.

"And so you were right." Bronwen leaned up enough to brush a smiling kiss to the top of her breast.

"So I was right, my destined hearts."

THE END

http://www.tonyaramagos.com

ABOUT THE AUTHOR

Bestselling author Tonya Ramagos spends much of her time daydreaming about one plot or another. Give her a cup of hazelnut flavored coffee and a keyboard and she is at her happiest. When she isn't writing, thinking about writing, or plotting what to write, she can be found taking on the mother role with her two boys and the husband, too. She enjoys taking long walks on the nature trails near her home in Chattanooga, TN, playing computer games, swinging on the playground, dancing, and curling up with a good book.

Siren Publishing, Inc.
www.SirenPublishing.com

Printed in the United States
154436LV00004B/103/P